Oscar and the Amazing Gravity Repellent is published by
Capstone Young Readers
A Capstone Imprint
1710 Roe Crest Drive
North Mankato, Minnesota 56003
www.capstoneyoungreaders.com

Library of Congress Cataloging-in-Publication Data
Peterson, Tina L., author.
  Oscar and the amazing gravity repellent / by Tina L. Peterson; cover
illustration, Xavier Bonet.
      pages cm
  Summary: Third-grader Oscar Schmidt is a klutz, totally lacking in
self-confidence, and gravity is his nemesis, all of which makes him
a target for the school bullies — until he and his friend Asha find
an abandoned train caboose and discover a bottle of Dr. Oopsie's
Amazing Gravity Repellent, and suddenly everything changes.

ISBN 978-1-4965-0000-7 (library binding)
ISBN 978-1-62370-244-1 (paper over board)
ISBN 978-1-4965-0160-8 (ebook pdf)
ISBN 978-1-62370-586-2 (reflowable epub)

1. Gravity--Juvenile fiction. 2. Clumsiness--Juvenile fiction. 3.
Self-confidence--Juvenile fiction. 4. Friendship--Juvenile fiction. 5.
Bullying--Juvenile fiction. 6. Elementary schools--Juvenile fiction. [1.
Gravity--Fiction. 2. Clumsiness--Fiction. 3. Self-confidence--Fiction. 4.
Friendship--Fiction. 5. Bullying--Fiction. 6. Schools--Fiction.] I. Bonet,
Xavier, 1979- illustrator. II. Title.
  PZ7.1.P46Os 2015
  [Fic]--dc23

                                    2014043421

Editor: Alison Deering
Designer: Alison Thiele

Printed in China
042015   008866RRDF15

OSCAR
and the AMAZING
Gravity
Repellent

by Tina L. Peterson

illustrations by Xavier Bonet

CAPSTONE YOUNG READERS
a capstone imprint

⤳ Chapter 1 ⤳

On a Thursday morning one month after he'd started third grade, Oscar Schmidt's teacher, Mrs. Faust, wrote a word on the board that would change his life forever — GRAVITY.

"Can anyone tell the class what this word means?" Mrs. Faust asked.

Oscar tried to look as small as possible so she wouldn't call on him. He thought the word had to do with graves and graveyards, but he knew he was probably wrong about that. Caitlin, the

1

teacher's pet, raised her hand high like she always did when a grown-up asked a question.

Mrs. Faust called on her. "Caitlin?"

"It's the natural force that keeps everything on the ground," Caitlin said primly.

Ordinarily Oscar found Caitlin rather annoying — she was such a know-it-all — but he sat up and paid attention when she said that.

"Very good, Caitlin," said Mrs. Faust. "Gravity is the force that pulls smaller objects toward a bigger object. The earth is a very big object, and its gravitational pull is what keeps everything from floating off the surface."

Mrs. Faust wrote GRAVITATIONAL PULL on the board, then turned back to her students. "Who can tell us who discovered gravity?" she asked.

Caitlin raised her hand again, but Mrs. Faust looked past her at the rest of the class. Oscar tried to make himself small again and was relieved when the teacher called on Asha, his best friend.

"Isaac Newton," Asha answered.

"That's right, Asha," said Mrs. Faust. "Isaac Newton was sitting under an apple tree one day when an apple fell off and hit him in the head."

That sounds like something that would happen to me, Oscar thought. He was sort of famous for his klutziness — he was always falling down, tripping on things, and generally making a mess.

"Newton thought about why the apple fell toward the ground," Mrs. Faust continued, "and then he realized that everything on earth fell down rather than up."

Oscar's eyes widened as he listened to his teacher's explanation. Suddenly he remembered something else Mrs. Faust had taught him: the earth is constantly spinning, and that's why the sun moves across the sky, creating a day and a night.

Mrs. Faust must have noticed how big his eyes were, because she looked over at him and smiled. Oscar never raised his hand in school, because he was scared of talking to most grown-ups. Sometimes his voice didn't seem to work when he wanted it to, and even if it did, he usually said something dumb.

"Oscar," said Mrs. Faust. Oscar sat up straight in his desk, and his throat tightened. "Can you think of another force that acts on objects without touching them?"

As his classmates waited for him to speak, Oscar racked his brain to think of the answer. They had been learning about forces all week, but he couldn't think of a single one. His throat was dry, and his face felt warm. Oscar said the first thing that came to mind.

"Um . . . wind?" he guessed. His voice squeaked when he spoke.

A few of his classmates laughed, but Mrs. Faust smiled. "Wind certainly acts on objects, Oscar," she agreed, "but it isn't quite the answer I was looking for."

Mrs. Faust began talking about magnets pulling on metal objects, but Oscar stopped listening. He felt silly and embarrassed. He put his arm down on his desk so he could hide his face in the crook of his elbow. Unfortunately his arm caught the corner of his open pencil case and sent it crashing to the floor. Along with a book. And a folder of workbook sheets.

There was an awful silence as all the other students stared at Oscar. They didn't laugh at him like they used to do in second grade, because their teacher had always shushed them immediately. Oscar almost wished they would laugh. At least then there would be another noise besides him scrambling to gather his things off the floor.

As Oscar struggled to collect pencils that had rolled under other kids' desks, he had a realization: the earth was spinning and pulling him to the ground at the same time. It was just like when he and Asha spun around and around in circles. They always fell over after a while. They couldn't help it — they were dizzy! If the earth made gravity and was always spinning, of course he fell over all the time. It was only natural!

The more Oscar thought about it, the more surprised he was that people weren't falling down all over the place. *How is anyone still standing at the end of the day, with all this crazy spinning and pulling going on around them?* he wondered.

That day at recess, Oscar watched the other kids on the playground very closely. The girls who played on the monkey bars definitely were pulled by gravity. They had to balance on the top of the bar carefully. When they leaned forward or back, they swung down toward the ground and went back and forth, back and forth until they stopped. But they didn't usually fall.

Maybe gravity doesn't like to get too close to girls, Oscar thought. *Maybe it knows that some of them have cooties.*

He watched a group of fourth graders play kickball. Gravity definitely worked on rubber balls. The ball flew, bounced high, bounced low, and then rolled. Oscar suspected that the balls he kicked in gym class had extra gravity added to them, because he could never get them to go very far.

* * *

Oscar had been a klutz for most of his life. His mom called him "accident-prone," which he didn't like because it sounded like something a doctor should fix.

Once, when he was about six years old, he'd decided that he wasn't accident-prone at all. He was actually a superhero who could fall over and break stuff in ways normal people couldn't. So he'd put on an old Halloween mask and taped a constuction-paper *S* to his chest. It stood for Super . . . something. He hadn't decided what.

With a tablecloth-cape tied around his neck, Oscar had zoomed around the house being Super-something. He'd run down to the basement where his dad had been painting a chair. Unfortunately, his cape had caught on the banister just as he'd rounded the corner.

"Gurf."

Stupid Super-something cape.

Whenever Oscar fell or tripped or broke something, he wanted to thrash his arms and kick his feet and yell, "Why? Whywhywhywhy! Why does stuff keep getting in my way? Why is it always *me* falling down and wrecking stuff? It's not FAIR!"

But Oscar knew if he did that, people would stare at him. And he *really* didn't like being stared at. So even if he hurt himself, he kept it to one word — or grunt, really — "Gurf."

After he had knocked over the paint can, Oscar had decided that maybe he wasn't a superhero after all. Maybe he was a rock star! He'd heard a story once about a rock star who'd broken his guitar while he was onstage.

I could do that! Oscar had thought. *I'd be great at that!*

His older sister, Gretchen, had liked the idea and said a rock star needed a T-shirt. She'd used a black marker to write TOUR OF DESTRUCTION in jagged letters on the back of Oscar's T-shirt. Then she'd treated him like a rock star for a whole day. She'd even asked him to autograph a piece of the lamp he'd broken that morning. Oscar had loved the attention; it made him feel like his accidents were cool instead of embarrassing. He'd sung along to the radio in the car for days after that, and his parents looked at him curiously.

Oscar had thought his rock star T-shirt was so cool that he'd worn it for two weeks straight until it got stinky. Finally his dad had thrown it in the laundry. But what Dad hadn't noticed was the brand-new red sock hiding in the washing machine. When it came out of the dryer, Oscar's TOUR OF DESTRUCTION T-shirt was pink.

Oscar had cried — very quietly — and thrown it in the trash.

Gretchen had told him that he didn't need a T-shirt to be a rock star. He just needed some greatest hits. She'd suggested that he document his tour to make sure his fans would remember it all. So Oscar had pulled out his brand-new box of colored pencils and started drawing all of his most memorable accidents.

The first thing on "Oscar's Greatest Hits" was the time he'd dropped his mom's phone into the fishbowl. He'd tried to show their fish, Herbert, a funny video of a cat getting caught in a sprinkler. He'd assumed Herbert disliked cats, since cats eat fish, and would find the video hilarious. But Herbert hadn't paid much attention, and Oscar had figured it was because he couldn't see the screen. So Oscar had pushed the phone right up to the surface of the water and then . . .

"Gurf."

Stupid slippery phone.

Then there was the time he'd dressed up as a mummy for Halloween. His costume had been *excellent*. He'd spent hours cutting old white sheets into long strips to wrap around his body. Oscar had decided to surprise Asha. Just before they were supposed to go trick-or-treating together, he'd tried to climb over the iron gate in front of Asha's house. One long mummy-strip had gotten caught, and then another, and then . . .

"Gurf."

Stupid pointy gate parts.

But Oscar's greatest-greatest hit was the butt print in the sidewalk. It had happened when his parents were fixing the cracked cement in front of their house. They'd just finished pouring wet concrete into wooden squares to make a new piece of sidewalk.

"Careful, Oscar. Stay away from the concrete," his mom had told him as she put orange tape around the new part.

"Careful, Oscar! Stay away from the concrete!" his dad had warned as he lined up orange cones in front of it.

Oscar had been nowhere near the concrete before it happened! He'd been poking around with a stick under a tree in the front yard. His stick had struck an anthill, and a swarm of angry ants had come rushing out. Oscar had been *very* startled. He'd fallen backward on the ground and started to scoot. But the ants had been persistent and very organized. They'd formed a long, black, moving chain that had followed Oscar as he scooted backward onto the sidewalk. He'd scooted under the orange tape, and past the orange cones, and then . . .

"Gurf."

Stupid wet concrete. Stupid ants.

* * *

Oscar thought about his TOUR OF DESTRUCTION greatest-hits drawings as he stood on the playground. That had been three years ago. The sidewalk in front of the house still had his butt print in it. Gretchen had made him autograph that too, so it said OSCAR in big letters right below the two round scoops where his butt had landed. The scoops filled with water when it rained, and sometimes he found worms and bugs in the puddles. Once last summer he'd tried to sit in them again, but he couldn't fit. His butt was already bigger than it used to be.

The TOUR OF DESTRUCTION had been fun, but most days, Oscar didn't feel like a rock star. He felt like an accident-prone klutz, and he got so tired of hearing, "Careful, Oscar!" He could only hope this was a phase he would grow out of someday, like his parents always said. But he didn't feel very sure.

~Chapter 2~

Oscar and Asha lived next door to each other, and they normally walked home from school together. On the day they learned about gravity, however, she had a dentist appointment, so he walked home by himself. Because he was still thinking about all he had learned, Oscar didn't pay attention to where he was going. He was too busy watching other people who were walking and carrying things.

How did they cope with all the spinning and pulling? he wondered. Gravity didn't seem to bother any of the grown-ups he saw. Maybe it was one of those things that you just learned to deal with as you got older, like boring dinner-table conversations.

Suddenly Oscar tripped and noticed that the path he was on had become awfully bumpy. He decided he should stop watching people and start watching where he was stepping. He, of all people, knew that sidewalks could be tricky. You had to watch them constantly, or they'd make you fall.

Oscar stared down at his feet as he walked. Sidewalk, sidewalk, crack, sidewalk, sidewalk, more cracks, patch of grass, broken sidewalk, bigger patch of grass.

When he looked up, he didn't recognize the street anymore. In the spaces where shops and houses should have been, there were scraggly trees and bushes. As he came around the corner of an old building, the sidewalk ended, and there were only weeds under his feet. In the hollow of a large tree nearby there was an empty potato chip bag, a dirty shoelace, and some dented aluminum cans.

Just then a raccoon scuttled out from beneath a bush, startling Oscar. The animal looked at him curiously. Oscar liked raccoons. He'd looked them up on the Internet once and learned that they were nocturnal, which meant they mostly came out at night when fewer people would see them. Raccoons seemed to like hiding, and Oscar could relate to that.

The animal turned away from him and skittered off, its striped tail wiggling back and forth. It disappeared into a concrete pipe that stuck out of a low hill hidden by weeds. Oscar picked his way through the weeds, crept carefully over the hill, and saw the pipe coming out the other side. Water trickled down from the opening into a tiny stream. Oscar followed the water, carefully making his way through prickly bushes.

After awhile the bushes and weeds grew taller, and Oscar stopped and looked around him. He was surrounded by green on all sides. The noises from the street were gone, replaced by the buzz of insects and the gentle trickle of the stream near his feet. Oscar had no idea where he was, but he was happy. If he fell or tripped, there was nothing to break and no one to stare at him.

Oscar continued pushing through the bushes. Just when it seemed they couldn't get any thicker, he broke through and stumbled upon a shady clearing. The trickle of water he'd been following joined a stream that flowed under an enormous tree. Fuzzy green-gray moss covered the trunk of the tree and its twisted, gnarled roots.

It occurred to Oscar that the tree would look incredibly creepy at night, but in the afternoon light, it seemed friendly and welcoming. Tiny yellow and purple flowers grew in the spaces between its roots, and long vines hung from its branches. Oscar wondered if he could swing from them. He pulled on one to test it and frowned as it came loose in his hand.

The air in the clearing was cool, and Oscar heard birds above his head singing "ooh-see, ooh-see." It was a birdcall he'd never heard before. Suddenly a scratching noise interrupted the birds' chatter. Oscar looked up and saw the raccoon sitting on a tree root a few yards in front of him. It stared at him out of black-masked eyes, then disappeared around the huge trunk of the tree. Oscar followed it, stepping carefully over one tree root, and another, and then . . .

"Gurf."

Stupid tree root. Oscar rolled over where he'd fallen, and sat up to think for a moment. *It's not*

the tree's fault, he thought, *and it isn't mine either.*
It's gravity.

The tree roots were so tangled and slippery that Oscar had a hard time finding his footing as he stood. He grabbed a handful of vines to pull himself up. Unfortunately for him, the vines came loose in his hand, and he fell to his knees.

Oscar sighed, sat back on the tree roots, and pulled at the tangle of vines that had fallen on his head. As he cleaned himself off, something just beyond the green leaves caught his eye. Behind the big tree, covered in moss and vines, was an old train caboose.

The caboose was huge, but it was almost completely hidden from view by the vines that wound around it. It was, without a doubt, the coolest and most interesting thing Oscar had ever seen. For a moment, all he could do was sit and stare as his imagination went wild with the possibilities of what might be inside.

Finally Oscar scrambled to his feet and started to pull at the vines along the bottom of the caboose. Crouching down, he saw a bunch of tree roots growing underneath the thing. *That's strange*, he thought.

He moved away so he could see the top of the caboose. Sure enough, the roots he'd seen at the bottom turned into a tree that continued straight through the roof. Either the caboose had fallen on the tree, or it had been sitting there for so long that a tree had grown up right through the middle of it. Branches stuck out every which way over the roof, and the birds singing "ooh-see, ooh-see" had made their nests among the leaves.

Oscar pulled more and more vines away from the side of the caboose. They tangled and caught on themselves as he yanked and twisted. He caught his breath when he saw what else was living there — a really big spider. The creature had made its web near the back corner.

Oscar was sort of afraid of spiders, so he decided to leave that part alone. He pulled and yanked and struggled to clear the rest of the vines. Although it was cool and shady in the clearing, sweat ran down his forehead, and he had to keep brushing damp hair out of his eyes.

After what seemed like an hour, Oscar stepped back and gasped at what he'd revealed. The caboose looked nothing like the trains that came through town. Those always had metal cars filled with coal or lumber. The caboose in the clearing was made mostly of wood, and the front of it was bent and splintered. It looked like it had run into something once upon a time, or been attacked with a really big hammer.

A row of narrow windows ran along the top of the car, but they were too high up for Oscar to see anything through them. Moss grew on the bottom edge where the sunlight probably didn't shine very often. The metal parts underneath, where the caboose would sit on the train track, were reddish-brown with rust.

Oscar crouched down and touched a chain that hung from the underside of the caboose. It was cool and damp, like it had been rained on for years and never dried off.

Oscar looked around the tree roots under the caboose. He wondered where the train tracks were. Sometimes he saw tracks in strange places, like in the middle of streets where he had never seen a train cross. His mother had told him that trolleys used to travel along the tracks. When people had stopped using the trolleys, they'd left the tracks where they were. But Oscar couldn't find any tracks around the caboose. So how on earth had it ended up in the clearing?

Standing up, Oscar studied the caboose. The paint was mostly faded and peeling, but the parts that had been protected by vines were bright red. On the side, the words "Dr. Oopsie's Traveling Tower of Tonics" were written in tall, fancy letters that swept up the side of the car. Below that was a painting of a man with a wiry mustache and a serious look on his face. He wore a black top hat and a suit with a bow tie. Old-fashioned round spectacles sat on the tip of his nose.

There were more words written on the lower corner of the caboose, partly hidden by moss. Oscar scraped at it with a stick. It read "J. E. Smith Novelties and Diversions, East Wyottasockim, New York."

New York! Oscar knew that was pretty far away from where he lived. The caboose must have traveled a really long way to get where it was.

He studied the words again. He didn't know what novelties and diversions were. The Popsicles he got from the ice cream truck in the summer said "frozen novelty" on the wrapper, but he doubted those were the same kinds of novelties that were inside the caboose.

Oscar looked around for a way to get inside. Bushes and tree roots blocked the end of the train car closest to him. He knew he had to go past the big spider to investigate the other end. Oscar took a deep breath and began to make his way over the shrubs and branches.

The spider's web reflected the afternoon sunlight poking through the trees. Oscar was pretty sure the spider was watching him as he approached the steps that led to the back end of the caboose. He had never moved so carefully in his life. If he tripped and fell into that web, he would yell a lot more than "Gurf."

Oscar reached the steps and pulled himself up onto the platform. There was a door with a latch and a small, high window. When Oscar stood on his tiptoes he could peer through it, but it was too murky with dirt to see much. He took the sleeve of his sweatshirt and wiped at the glass until he could see better. Even then, it was so dark inside the caboose that Oscar couldn't see much more than brown, blurry shapes.

In the middle of the caboose stood something huge, so tall that it reached from the floor to the ceiling. Oscar didn't believe in monsters, but that was before he'd seen this one. It startled him so much that he fell backward into the bushes behind the train car.

"AAUGH!" Oscar yelped. It had been so long since he had actually shouted; he was as surprised as the birds overhead. They stopped singing "ooh-see" and called out "Fwaaa! Fwaaa!" as they flew away.

Oscar scrambled out from the bushes and shook his arms and legs quickly as he hopped up and down. "No spiders, no spiders, spiders, go AWAY!" he hollered. He suddenly stopped, embarrassed. He'd startled himself with the sound of his own voice, and he was glad no one was there to stare at him.

It was so quiet near the caboose, which made Oscar wonder about the monster inside. Maybe it wasn't real, or maybe it was standing very still, waiting for him. The big spider around the corner was definitely real, though. There were so many things to fear that Oscar couldn't decide what the best reason to be scared was. He crouched down and tucked the bottoms of his pants into his socks. This made him feel a tiny bit braver.

As he fixed his socks, Oscar again noticed the tree roots under the caboose. He stood up and tracked the line of the tree upward with his eyes. Then it hit him — the tree inside looked an awful lot like a monster.

Oscar smacked his forehead and made a face. He let out a breath he didn't realize he'd been holding and again climbed up the steps to the back of the caboose. He grabbed the latch and tried to open it, but it was stuck closed with rust. He pulled at it, up and down and back and forth, and whacked at it with a stick. The latch would not budge.

Defeated, Oscar hung his head and sighed loudly. The sun was going down, and he didn't want to be in the clearing once the big tree turned *really* scary. He vowed to come back tomorrow and figure out a way to get into the caboose.

Oscar climbed carefully down the steps and ran past the spider web. He felt proud of himself. He had only fallen twice, and the last time was only because the tree-trunk-monster had scared him. That could have happened to anyone. Even Asha, who was pretty brave, probably would have been scared too.

Oscar filled his head with plans to get inside the caboose, and he got very excited about returning the next day. He started to skip and hop over the tree roots, one and then another and then . . .

"Gurf."

Stupid tree root. Stupid gravity.

～Chapter 3～

Oscar wasn't interested in dinner that night. He was too excited about his discovery to eat. Instead, he made a science experiment of his food. Would gravity affect a meatball? He held it above the mound of spaghetti and let go of it. *Splat!* Spots of tomato sauce were all over his sweatshirt and the tablecloth.

Yup, gravity worked on meatballs. Now, what about the milk? Oscar leaned in and held his milk glass over the plate. He began to tilt it slowly so that . . .

"Oscar!" his mother shouted.

Oscar sat straight up, startled, and looked at his mother. She looked a lot like him — or rather, he looked like her. They had the same brown eyes, the same freckles, and the same nose that turned up a little at the end. But he'd always thought the face looked better on her — pretty, even. Except now it looked more irritated than anything else.

"What are you doing?" Mom asked. "Besides making a mess?"

"I'm testing gravity," Oscar replied calmly. He didn't get nervous talking to his parents like he did with other grown-ups. But he still didn't like answering a lot of questions. He looked down at his plate again and tried to appear busy.

"Gravity?" his mother repeated.

"We learned about it in school today," Oscar explained, turning a meatball around with his fork. He knew that would impress them. His parents were always asking him what he learned in school that day. If he made playing with his food sound like a learning experience, he might not get in as much trouble for making a mess.

"Oh," his mother said. She looked at his father with a small smile on her face. "Gravity. That's very interesting, Oscar. What did you learn about it?"

Ugh. Whenever he said he'd learned something in school, his mom and dad asked him *tons* of questions about it. He wished he could just test his meatballs and milk in peace.

"Um," he began, "Mrs. Faust said that gravity comes from the earth . . . because it's bigger than we are. So we stick to it. And that's why. . . when you hold something up and drop it, it falls."

Oscar hoped he wouldn't have to say any more. He wanted to test another meatball, but he decided to wait until his parents weren't watching him quite so closely.

"That's true," his father said, nodding. "And the heavier an object is, the faster it drops."

Oscar was surprised by how interested his father sounded. They didn't usually have a lot in common, even though relatives always said he was the spitting image of his father, whatever that meant. Dad was tall, and Oscar was short. Dad was good at baseball, and Oscar could barely swing a bat without hitting something *other* than the ball.

"Wait, no," his mother said, tilting her head to the side. She always did that when she was thinking. "Doesn't everything fall at the same speed after a while?"

"No, no, think about it," his father said. "If I drop a feather and a bowling ball, which will hit the ground sooner?"

"The bowling ball, of course, but that's because . . ." Mom started to say.

"Because it's heavier," Dad finished.

Mom shook her head. "No, it's because the feather catches in the air. It's friction."

"And because the bowling ball is heavier," his father said, sitting back and smiling.

Oscar's mother crossed her arms and narrowed her eyes, and he could tell she was getting ready to debate with his father. "Yes, it's heavier, but doesn't everything fall at the same speed after a certain point? It's called, oh, what is it?" She snapped her fingers. "Terminal velocity."

"Well, yes, but a bowling ball is still going to . . ."

Oscar tuned his parents out. They could go on like this *forever*. It was amazing how grown-ups could make something so interesting sound so boring. Across the table, Gretchen tapped away at her phone and giggled. She looked like a perfect combination of both of their parents, and sometimes that made Oscar jealous. But he liked his big sister, even though she hadn't talked to him much since she got a new phone.

Oscar was glad his parents were so involved in their debate, because that meant they didn't notice when he started pouring milk onto his plate. It pooled in the spaces underneath his meatballs and spaghetti. Next he stood his fork up on the table and let it go — it toppled backward, just like Oscar had toppled off the caboose. He was satisfied with the experiment. Gravity seemed to work pretty well on everything at the table.

Oscar studied his plate. At this point, his food was looking kind of gross. He definitely didn't feel like eating it now. "May I be excused?" he asked.

Gretchen glanced at his plate and frowned. Usually their parents made them finish at least half their meal before they were allowed to get up. But Mom and Dad were still talking excitedly about the mass of a feather, so they didn't pay any attention to Oscar's meatball-and-milk mess.

* * *

After dinner, Oscar felt restless. He used the computer in the kitchen and did an Internet search on gravity. One website said that gravity was the weakest of the four forces of nature. That was a bit hard to believe, considering how hard it made him fall when he tripped.

I hope I never have to deal with the other three, Oscar thought.

He also found a lot of stuff about Isaac Newton and some complicated math equations. The math stuff was confusing, so Oscar decided to look up the name he'd seen on the caboose instead. When he typed in "Dr. Oopsie" he found a bunch of websites, but none of them had anything to do with tonics or cabooses. Oscar sighed. Sometimes the Internet was no help at all.

After he brushed his teeth and got into bed, Oscar lay awake for a long time staring at the ceiling. He plotted and planned how he would get into the caboose the next day. Eventually he drifted off to sleep, his mind full of thoughts about Dr. Oopsie and his novelties and diversions. But right before he fell asleep, he came up with a plan.

⌒Chapter 4⌒

The next morning, Oscar emptied his coin jar into his pockets. He hoped it would be enough for his plan. His pants jangled with pennies and nickels and dimes and quarters as he skipped happily to school. He slowed down and walked carefully over the cracked parts of the sidewalk. He tripped over these cracks at least once a week, and he didn't want to spill any of the money.

As he came around the last corner before school, Oscar saw a group of older boys practicing skateboard tricks off the curb. They went to the same middle school as Gretchen, and Oscar sometimes saw them spraying words on fences with cans of paint. The shortest one was named Zach. He was in sixth grade, and he was a bully. Oscar knew all that from Gretchen, but he didn't know how mean the kid was. He might be steal-his-money-and-run mean, or he might be hit-him-in-the-face mean.

Oscar kept his head down and walked slowly as he tried to figure out how to get past them. Should he cross the street to the other side and risk looking like he was scared of them? (He was, of course!) Or should he walk right by them and try to look as tough as possible? Whatever he did would draw attention.

He decided to try walking by them. As he approached, Oscar clenched his fists and tried to look mean. It didn't work at all. He still looked like Oscar Schmidt, a not-remotely-mean third grader with too many freckles and hair that always stuck up in the back.

Zach noticed him first. "Hey, dude!" the older boy called. "Hey, I'm talking to YOU!"

Oscar felt a tiny bit of relief that Zach didn't know his name. A few of the fourth graders at his school sometimes called him "Oscar Mayer" and made dumb jokes about hot dogs. Still, Oscar wasn't sure how he should react. He knew smiling or saying, "Hey, dude," back would only open him up to more teasing, so he ignored Zach and kept walking.

"Aw, he can't talk, guys! Isn't that sad?" Zach taunted. "He must have snot for brains. Poor snotbrain."

The other boys laughed and started making snot jokes.

"Hey, when you blow your nose, do you get even stupider?"

"Hey, when you pick your nose, do you eat it, so it'll go back in and you won't get any dumber?"

Zach and his friends cackled and gave each other high fives.

Oscar's face grew hot and his heart beat in his ears, but he kept walking. He was about to pass Zach when all of a sudden he fell flat on his face. One of the boys must have tripped him, because he had been watching his feet so carefully.

As Oscar hit the sidewalk, the change in his pockets spilled out and rolled everywhere. He tasted blood and felt tears welling up in his eyes. He was so afraid of drawing attention to himself that he didn't even grunt "Gurf" when he fell.

"Whoa, check it out. Snotbrain is a piggy bank!" Zach shouted. He and the other boys all raced to grab the change off the ground.

Oscar felt his face get hot — he needed that money for his plan! He began to yell and kick his feet out in all directions. He hadn't made that much noise in years, and he didn't know where it had come from.

It must have surprised the boys too, because they backed away and started to laugh nervously.

"Whoa, there's something seriously wrong with Snotbrain," Zach said to his friends. "Better not touch his money, or you might catch whatever he has. C'mon guys, let's get away from this loser."

The bully dropped the coins he'd grabbed, and the others did the same. They grabbed their skateboards and headed off down the street together, laughing and punching each other's shoulders.

Oscar pulled himself up on his hands and knees and frantically collected his money off the ground. Two dimes had fallen into a sewer grate, and he couldn't reach them. His face burned in anger at Zach and the other boys, and his hands stung from hitting the sidewalk when he fell.

Stupid bullies. Stupid gravity.

After he'd gathered the coins, Oscar got to his feet and continued his walk to school. He tried to stop the hot tears that threatened to spill from his eyes. He decided to think about the caboose instead.

That worked. By the time he walked into his classroom, Oscar had a small, determined smile on his face. Even the bully, and the lost dimes, and the pain in his hands and chin couldn't ruin his mood that morning. He was too excited about his plan.

* * *

Mrs. Faust showed them a video of astronauts on the moon. The men bounced gently along, seeming to walk in slow motion. Oscar stared at them with his mouth hanging open.

"What's different about the surface of the moon?" Mrs. Faust asked. "Why do the astronauts move the way they do?"

Caitlin had all the answers again, but this time Oscar listened closely instead of rolling his eyes.

"Gravity is different on different planets . . . or moons," Caitlin said. "There's less gravity on the moon, so the astronauts are lighter there."

"That's right, Caitlin," said Mrs. Faust.

Oscar stared out the window at the first graders, who were already having recess. *Maybe I would trip and fall less on another planet with less gravity*, he thought.

Just then, Asha poked him in the ribs to get his attention. Oscar jumped in his seat, startled, and some of the coins fell out of his pockets onto the floor. A few of his classmates laughed, but Mrs. Faust quieted them with a stern look.

Asha waited until he had retrieved the coins, then gently poked him again. "What are you doing after school?" she whispered.

Oscar thought for a moment. He wasn't ready to share the caboose until he had opened it himself. He and Asha usually did everything together, and he didn't want to hurt her feelings by not inviting her along. In this case, he decided it would be okay to tell a tiny lie.

"I have to go to the dentist," he whispered back.

Asha made a face at him, but didn't say anything else. Oscar hoped she wouldn't notice him watching the clock, waiting for school to be over so he could put his plan into action.

~Chapter 5~

When the last bell finally rang, Oscar ran to get his backpack and managed to beat all his classmates out the door. He was heading down the front steps of the school when Asha caught up to him, huffing and puffing.

"Why are you running?" she asked.

Oscar hesitated. "I have to go to my dad's office, so he can drive me to my appointment," he said, starting to walk away.

"But your dad's office is that way," Asha called out, pointing in the opposite direction. "And you went to the dentist a few weeks ago."

Geez, does she remember everything? Oscar thought. Usually he liked how smart Asha was. She knew a lot of big words, she had great ideas for adventures, and she could fix a lot of things. But today he wished he was best friends with someone a little less observant. Someone like Trent, the kid who came to school every day with his shirt inside out.

Oscar walked back over to Asha and stood for a moment, thinking. Then he pulled her around a corner where there were no other kids. He liked talking with Asha more than with anyone else, but only when no one else could hear him.

"Okay," he admitted. "I'm not going to the dentist."

"I knew it!" Asha cried. "Where are you going? Can I —"

"Shhhh!" Oscar whispered, covering her mouth with his hand.

"Blech!" Asha said, pushing it away. "Your hand smells like old pennies." She leaned in and whispered, "Where are you going?"

Oscar took a deep breath. "I can't tell you today, but I'll tell you soon."

"How soon?"

"Very soon. You just have to trust me."

Asha's eyes widened. "Is it cool?"

"It's *so* cool," Oscar replied.

"I want to come with you!" Asha exclaimed.

"Shhhhh! You can't today. But soon, I promise."

Asha pouted and stomped away around the corner, but Oscar knew she wouldn't follow him. She was smart, but she wasn't nosy.

As soon as Asha was out of sight, Oscar turned in the other direction and started walking as quickly as he could to Art's Hardware. He made it there in no time and stepped inside. The space was cool and smelled like sawdust and fresh paint.

Oscar's parents had been customers of the small store for years, and he loved to shop with them there. A hardware store didn't have a lot of delicate, breakable things, so he rarely heard anyone say, "Careful, Oscar!" He loved to explore the narrow aisles and to imagine what all the tools, fixtures, and fasteners were used for.

Oscar had never visited the store without his parents, but the man behind the counter — possibly Art himself — recognized him and smiled. "Hello, there," the man said. He looked older than Oscar's grandmother and had wire-rimmed eyeglasses perched on the tip of his nose.

Oscar took a deep breath and stood up as tall as he could. He had never spoken to this man before, because his parents had always done the talking.

The man raised his eyebrows and pointed to the scrape on Oscar's chin. "Did you take a little tumble?" he asked.

For a moment Oscar was confused. He had forgotten all about the bully and his friends that morning. Then he touched his chin and remembered. "Oh, this? It doesn't hurt," he said quietly, shaking his head. He reminded himself to be polite to the man. "Um . . . sir," he began, "do you have anything that can open a . . . thing that's rusty?"

"What kind of a thing?" the man asked. "A lock?"

"No, um . . ." Oscar hesitated. What if the man figured out what he was trying to do? What if he got in trouble for breaking into the old caboose? He'd already told one lie today, and he didn't feel like telling another one, especially to a grown-up.

Oscar decided to tell a little bit of the truth — only what was important. He took a deep breath. "It's a . . . latch," he said finally. "It's rusted shut." He smiled at the man, hoping there would be no more questions.

"A rusty latch . . ." The man scratched his chin. He seemed satisfied with that explanation.

As Oscar stood with the polite smile frozen on his face, the man disappeared down an aisle. He returned a moment later holding a small can with a nozzle on top.

"This should do the trick, son," the man said. "Shake the can first, then spray it all over the latch. Make sure to really get it into the cracks and corners. Then wait for a few minutes and try to open it."

"Okay. I'll do that," Oscar said, nodding. His voice sounded louder somehow — stronger. He felt very grown-up, chatting with the man about a problem to solve.

"Be very careful with it, young man," the man warned, leaning across the counter and peering at Oscar over the top of his glasses. "Make sure you don't spray it in your nose, or your mouth, or your eyes."

That made Oscar feel like a kid again. "Oh, yes, certainly . . . I mean, no, I certainly won't," he said, stuttering a bit but shaking his head seriously.

The man leaned back and smiled.

"How much is it?" Oscar asked in a small voice.

"Let's see here," the man said, squinting at the can. "Two dollars and ninety-nine cents. With tax, that's three-twenty."

Oscar carefully scooped the change out of his pockets and piled it on the counter. The man chuckled, rested his elbows on the counter, and began counting the money. He muttered numbers and sorted the coins into stacks.

"Hmm. Three dollars, six cents," the man said. "You're a little short. You need another fourteen cents."

Oscar's face grew hot. His piggy bank was empty. He thought of the two dimes that had fallen in the sewer that morning and felt angry all over again at Zach and his friends.

He was embarrassed and couldn't look the man in the face. Instead Oscar stared down at the counter, wondering what would happen next.

"You know what?" the man said after a moment. "The rest is on the house. Be sure and let me know if you get it open."

Oscar looked up, startled. Had he told the man about the caboose itself? He couldn't remember how much he'd said. He must have looked confused, because the man smiled and spoke again, gently.

"The latch. Let me know if you get the latch open."

Oscar smiled in relief. "I will," he agreed. "Thank you." He took the small paper bag the man handed to him, along with a receipt for the purchase. Then he walked out of the store, feeling like a grown-up again.

～Chapter 6～

Oscar started down the street in the direction of the clearing. After a few blocks, he stopped and looked around. This wasn't right. He turned down another street and walked a block or two. Nothing looked familiar. There were too many shops, too many houses, and too many people. The street that led to the clearing had been empty. But where was it?

Every alleyway and every shortcut Oscar could find all led to the same street. Soon he realized he was seeing the same houses again and again — he was going in circles.

Oscar sat down on a bench and dropped his chin in his hands. What if he had dreamed the whole thing? And if it was a dream, what if he could never have the same one again? That's how it always was with good dreams. They only came once, and when you woke up, they were gone. You could try to go back to sleep, to remember where the dream had left off, but you could never find it again.

Oscar's lower lip began to quiver. *No*, he thought, *I won't cry. It's just a stupid caboose. An old, stupid caboose. An ugly, old, stupid caboose. An ugly, old, stupid caboose that might be full of stuff. Old stuff. Old, fascinating stuff.*

With that thought, he began crying for real. Tears leaked out of the corners of his eyes and ran down his cheeks before he could wipe them away. He tried not to make any noise, and he hoped no one was watching.

Oscar pulled himself up from the bench, quietly hiccuping as he tried to stop crying. The paper bag from the hardware store fell to the ground. He left it where it was and walked slowly along the sidewalk, his head hanging low. He kicked a small pebble, just because he felt like kicking something.

PWOCK! The pebble hit a Dumpster. A raccoon scurried out from beneath it and looked at Oscar accusingly, as if he had interrupted its lunch or maybe a nap. The raccoon disappeared into some nearby bushes. Oscar wondered if it was the same animal he had seen before. He had a strange feeling he should follow it, so he did.

Beyond the bushes was a path Oscar had never seen before. It didn't look like the way to the clearing, but he decided to see where it led. Soon the raccoon vanished into a thicket. It was full of brambles that looked prickly and was probably full of spiders. Oscar picked his way past some nearby bushes that seemed a bit friendlier. He felt the ground slope upward, and then suddenly, it disappeared beneath his feet.

"Gurf."

Stupid gravity.

It all happened so quickly. Oscar tumbled through the bushes down a small hill. When he reached the bottom, he stood up and brushed himself off, wincing as he touched his skinned elbows. Between his tumble and his encounter with the bully that morning, Oscar knew he would look worse than usual when he got home that day. He hoped his parents wouldn't ask too many questions.

After he untangled himself from the bushes, Oscar realized where he was — the clearing!

His clearing! It was just as he remembered. The stream flowed under the enormous tree, the yellow and purple flowers seemed to smile, and the birds sang "ooh-see, ooh-see."

Oscar ran around the tree and saw the old caboose. It seemed brighter and bigger than it had the day before. *It isn't hidden anymore*, he thought. *I cleared away too many vines. I better cover it up again before I leave, so no one else finds it.*

He ran to the far end of the caboose and scrambled up the steps to the back door. He was so excited he forgot to be afraid of the big spider in the corner. But when he went to open the latch, he remembered that he'd dropped the bag from the hardware store.

Leaving his backpack on the train steps, Oscar ran out of the clearing and back up the hill as fast as he could. On his way back to the train, he only tripped once. But he was so glad to have found the old caboose again that he barely noticed.

Paper bag in hand, Oscar raced up the steps to the door. He followed the directions the man at the hardware store had given him and sprayed the liquid all over the latch, especially on the corners and cracks. Now all he could do was wait.

How long is this going to take? Oscar wondered. *What did the man say?*

He sat down on the steps and fidgeted. He couldn't remember the last time he'd been this excited. Maybe Christmas morning two years ago, when he was seven. He'd gotten a new bike that year, and it had been beautiful. First he'd had to wait to unwrap the huge box, and *then* he'd had to wait for his parents to assemble it. Oscar had jumped all over the house, bouncing off walls and furniture, while his parents had hollered, "Calm down!" and, "Careful, Oscar!" But that morning didn't even compare to this; he was sure the caboose had something interesting or scary or both inside of it.

How long has it been? Oscar thought. It felt like an hour had passed, but it was probably more like two minutes. He couldn't wait any longer.

Oscar stood up and grabbed the latch with both hands. He jiggled it gently, then a bit harder. The latch squeaked. He grabbed the can and sprayed more of the liquid into the part that squeaked. He jiggled it again, and it moved a quarter of an inch. He pulled and pushed, jiggled and wiggled and yanked until the latch released. *SCREEAAAK!*

Overhead, the "ooh-see" birds flew away, startled by the noise. It was so quiet that Oscar could hear his own heartbeat. He examined the door. It didn't swing back and forth like the ones at home. Instead, it slid to the side. The whole thing was sticky with rust and incredibly heavy, but Oscar managed to open it. Then he stepped inside and gasped at what he saw.

The caboose's interior was even bigger than it had looked from the outside. The ceiling curved high above Oscar's head. The car was so wide he could lie down on the floor with his arms stretched out and not touch the walls on either side. The whole hardware store could have fit inside it.

The high windows were thick with dirt, and almost no light came through them. But the sun streamed in through the open door, providing just enough light for Oscar to see. The walls were covered in green paper that peeled and curled away in the corners, and red velvet curtains hung along one side. Against the other wall stood a long glass case, the kind amusement park arcades used to display prizes. But it was covered in so much dust that Oscar couldn't see what was inside.

Oscar marveled at the tree that had grown up through the middle of the caboose. The wooden floorboards were bent and broken where the tree had poked up through the bottom, and there was a huge hole in the ceiling where the tree stuck out. Vines had filled in the gap and hung down the trunk of the tree. Oscar had always wanted a tree house, and suddenly it felt like he had the coolest one in the world.

In the far corner, near the red curtains, there was a wooden cutout of a man wearing a top hat and an old-fashioned suit. It was the same man painted on the side of the caboose. Next to the cutout was a sign that read: *Dr. Zebediah Phonicious Oopsilon has a degree in the medical arts from Oxfortus University. He is a kindly fellow, beloved by animals and children and known to his many friends as Dr. Oopsie.*

Oscar made his way around the tree to investigate the other end of the caboose. Along one wall stood a chest of tiny drawers, each one only a few inches wide. He opened one and found a metal tool lying on a green velvet cushion. It looked like the tongs his mother used to turn over chicken drumsticks when she was cooking, but it had long, sharp tines like a fork at each end.

Oscar slid open a different drawer and found a tiny magnifying glass at the end of a long metal handle. In another drawer he found one of those devices doctors put in their ears to listen to your heart. In the drawer below that, he found a small knife. He carefully picked it up and looked closely at the reddish-brown rust on its blade.

He shivered and inhaled sharply, then jumped at the sound his breath made in the quiet of the old caboose. His hands shook a little as he placed the knife back in its drawer and slid the drawer closed.

At the far end of the train car, opposite the door, there was another red curtain. Suddenly Oscar started to worry about what might be behind it. He wished he'd brought Asha along with him in case there was a really big spider or a . . . a what? He could imagine so many scary things. He opened the first drawer again and picked up the pointy fork tongs. If a bogeyman was hiding behind the curtain, at least Oscar would have a fighting chance.

He walked toward the far end of the caboose, and the floorboards squeaked under his feet. His heart beat loudly in his ears as he grabbed the edge of the curtain with one hand, holding the tongs in the other. He flung the curtain back and let loose a riotous cloud of dust and moths, which fluttered around him in a panic. Oscar shrank away and hid his face in the crook of his elbow while he waited for the moths to scatter.

When the coast was clear, Oscar dropped his arm, relieved — but a bit disappointed — at what he saw. It looked like someone's bedroom. Small, high windows let a tiny bit of light into the space. There was a narrow bed with a quilt neatly tucked around the edges.

Sitting on the table next to the bed was a lamp unlike any Oscar had ever seen. It was made of glass and metal, and there was brownish liquid in the bottom. Something that looked like a shoestring, blackened at the top, dangled down into the liquid. Next to the lamp was a framed photograph of an unsmiling woman. Her eyes looked strange, as if she had blinked or moved right as the picture was taken. She looked sad and blurry, the way people often did in old black-and-white photos.

A bit bored with what he found in the bedroom, Oscar went back through the curtain into the main room and stood in front of the long glass display case. The glass was so caked with dust that there could have been a mummy in there, and Oscar wouldn't have seen it. He shuddered at the thought. Maybe he didn't want to look inside after all.

What's scarier, Oscar wondered, *something you can't see that might be only in your imagination, or something very real that you can look right at?*

His imagination was doing a good job coming up with terrifying possibilities, so Oscar decided that what was real couldn't be any worse. He took the sleeve of his sweatshirt and rubbed it in a small circle until he could see through the glass.

Then he leaned over and peered into the case. In the murky darkness he saw something that widened his eyes and quickened his heartbeat.

Sitting on a shelf inside the case was a small brown bottle. Its label, faded and peeling around the edges, read DR. OOPSIE'S AMAZING GRAVITY REPELLENT.

⌒Chapter 7⌒

Oscar's mind raced as he stared at the bottle. He knew he had just made a very important discovery. *Insect repellent keeps bugs from biting me*, he thought, *and the tent we sleep in when we're camping is water-repellent. If the tent keeps water away, then gravity repellent must . . .*

His heart beat faster as he realized what the contents of the little bottle might be able to do. He felt like that boy Charlie in the book about the chocolate factory when he found a golden ticket. Unfortunately, Oscar's golden ticket was in a locked glass case. And as far as he could tell, there was no way in. He didn't want to break the glass, because he feared damaging the potentially precious bottle.

Asha, Oscar thought. *She'll know what to do.* He rushed out of the train car, closed the door carefully behind him, and hopped down to the ground.

As he started up through the tangle of bushes, Oscar stopped and looked back at Dr. Oopsie's old caboose. Now that he had pulled away so many of the vines, the train car looked terribly exposed in the light of day. Its red paint seemed brighter, and he worried it would be seen by someone through the trees. He was especially nervous that Zach and his friends might find it. He'd seen them do dumb things like break windows in old buildings. If they found Oscar's treasure, there was no telling what they might do to it.

He needed to cover the caboose up again. Oscar started pulling vines up from the floor of the clearing and tossing them as high as he could so they would drape over its side. It was no easy task. Most of them slipped right back off, because he couldn't throw them high enough to catch on anything.

He stood puzzling for a few minutes about how to get the vines to stay in place. Then he remembered the ladder he'd seen at the rear of the caboose. It led up to the roof of the car. Oscar decided to climb it. He knew it was a spectacularly bad idea for a klutzy person like him to get on top of a rickety old thing like the caboose. But he was so afraid that the bullies would find his treasure that he was willing to take a risk to protect it.

Oscar's concentration was fierce as he climbed the ladder to the top of the caboose. He crawled slowly around on the roof, pushing vines over the edge so they draped down the side.

Suddenly, his sneaker slipped on some wet leaves, and his leg shot out over the side. He clutched a tree branch that stuck through the roof and took a deep breath. If he fell and broke his leg, it could be days, maybe weeks, before anyone would find him. He would never get to unlock the glass case inside.

Slowly and carefully, Oscar crawled back to the ladder and climbed down. The vines he had already pushed over the side would have to be enough. The camouflage wasn't perfect, but the caboose was much less visible than it had been before.

Satisfied that his treasure was protected, Oscar raced out of the clearing and headed toward Asha's house. He was so preoccupied thinking about the gravity repellent that he paid little attention to where he put his feet. In fact, he was so happy that he started to skip. Oscar knew skipping was another spectacularly bad idea. It isn't wise for a klutzy person to skip, even in the best and most alert of moods.

As Oscar walked down the sidewalk, the toe of his sneaker caught a crack in the cement and then . . .

"Gurf."

Stupid gravity.

The universe was rubbing it in his face after his discovery.

Asha sat on the front steps of her house reading a book. She looked up when she heard his grunt. "Oscar?"

"Over here," Oscar groaned, reaching one hand over the fence.

Asha hurried over and helped him up. She noticed his dirt-smeared sweatshirt and his dusty hair and laughed. "What have you been doing? You're an even bigger mess now than you were at school."

Oscar didn't mind when Asha laughed at his klutziness. He knew she didn't do it to be mean — not like some of the other kids.

"Remember the thing I told you about earlier?" Oscar asked.

"Yeah?"

"Do you want to see it?"

"What is it?" Asha's eyes widened.

"It's hard to describe. You should just come see it." Oscar thought about the glass case, and a great idea occurred to him. "Hey," he added excitedly, "do you still have tools to pick a lock?"

"Shhh!" Asha whispered, putting her finger to her lips. She looked over her shoulder toward her house. "What do you think I am? I don't do that kind of thing."

Oscar crossed his arms and raised one eyebrow.

"Okay, once," Asha admitted. "But that was for a genealogy project."

The previous summer Asha had been convinced that her parents were hiding a twin sister from her. She and Oscar had figured the proof had to be in her parents' filing cabinet, so she'd picked the lock on it. They'd been very disappointed to find nothing but old tax forms and passports inside.

"Whatever," Oscar said, rolling his eyes. Asha liked to use big words to make the things that she did sound more important. "I need you to pick another lock."

Asha grinned and ran inside to get her tools. Then she followed Oscar around the corner, and they headed to the clearing.

~Chapter 8~

For the third time, Oscar got lost trying to find the caboose. He saw the tree with trash sitting in its hollow, but nothing else looked familiar. Asha stood several feet away, watching him and shifting her weight from one foot to the other.

Oscar turned around and around, looking in all directions. In his frustration, he kicked a cardboard box that was lying on its side next to the tree. To his surprise, a raccoon skittered out of it and ran past him. The animal disappeared into a concrete pipe poking out of a small hill that Oscar could have sworn hadn't been there a moment ago.

"It's this way," he shouted to Asha. Oscar ran over the small hill with Asha following him, and soon they were standing in the clearing under the big tree.

"Isn't it great?" Oscar panted, out of breath with excitement.

Asha looked confused. "It's a . . . nice tree," she began, "but what did you want me to unlock?"

"Oh!" Oscar exclaimed. He ran over to the caboose, feeling proud that he had hidden it so well even Asha hadn't noticed it. "It's this!" He lifted up one of the vines.

Asha walked over to where he stood, her eyes wide. "Wow!" she cried as she took in the size of the thing. "What is it?"

"I think it's an old doctor's office or something," Oscar said. He lifted up the vines from Dr. Oopsie's picture. "See, this guy was a doctor. Come on, it's even cooler inside."

Oscar led her to the back of the caboose, and they climbed up the steps. "The latch was rusted shut, but I put some of this stuff on it and I got it open," he said proudly, showing her the can from the hardware store. He slid open the door and stood to the side so Asha could see. She gasped and jumped back. "Don't worry, it's just a tree," he told her wisely.

Asha stepped into the caboose carefully. Oscar grinned as she looked around, exclaiming about how interesting everything was. He giggled as she pulled back the curtain and swatted away the startled moths.

As she made her way around the rest of the caboose, Asha discovered something Oscar hadn't noticed: a cupboard full of glass jars and tubes and small rubber corks.

"It looks like a laboratory," Asha said, picking up a thin glass tube and examining it. "Maybe that guy painted on the side was a scientist or something."

"But it says he's a doctor," Oscar said.

"A scientist can be a different kind of doctor," Asha said. Oscar shrugged. Asha's parents were very smart and worked at a university. He figured she was probably right about these things.

On the top shelf of the cupboard sat several jars, all of which had things floating in them. Asha took out one of the jars and held it up to the light, and she and Oscar peered at its contents. A dead rat floated inside, its thick tail curled up in the bottom.

"EWWW!" they both exclaimed.

Oscar was proud he had explored the caboose by himself first, but he had to give Asha credit. She was much braver than most of the girls in their school — and most of the boys too. Oscar liked to think he would have picked up the rat jar himself, but he wasn't sure.

"It must be in formaldehyde," Asha said.

"What's that?" Oscar said, wrinkling his nose.

"It keeps dead things from decaying," she explained. "My mom uses it in her lab. She says it preserves things so she can run tests on them."

"Well," Oscar said, "if this guy was a scientist, maybe he did tests on the rat."

Asha put the rat jar back in the cupboard. She and Oscar leaned closer to get a better look at what was in the other glass containers. Toward the back was a small jar with something familiar-looking suspended inside. Their eyes widened as they realized what it was — a finger.

"AUUUGH!" both kids screamed. They slammed the cupboard door shut and fell backward, scooting away from it as if they expected something to come out and bite them.

"Was that a . . . a finger?" Oscar asked, his eyes wide. "Where did it come from?"

"I don't know, but I don't want to reach in there and find out," Asha said.

Oscar didn't want to either. He was secretly glad it had scared her too.

Asha slowly stood up, brushed off her shorts, and walked over to the wooden cutout of Dr. Oopsie. She crossed her arms and peered at the figure for a while. "This place is kind of creepy," she finally said, turning back to Oscar. "I can't tell if he's a good doctor or a bad one. I don't know if I want to see what else is in here."

"No, you have to," Oscar said. "You haven't seen the coolest thing. It's in here." He scrambled to his feet and went over to the long glass display case that held the bottle of gravity repellent. He crouched down and pointed to the spot he'd cleaned off earlier with his sweatshirt. Asha crouched next to him and looked inside.

"Repellent keeps something away, right?" Oscar said, watching her face for a reaction. He was pretty sure that was correct, but he wanted a second opinion.

Asha nodded. "Yeah, I think so. Insect repellent keeps bugs off of you, so . . ." she said, slowly trailed off.

"So gravity repellent must keep gravity away from you!" Oscar exclaimed. "Right?"

Asha shrugged her shoulders. "Yeah, but . . . it probably doesn't even work."

Oscar felt stung by Asha's words. He stood up slowly. This thought hadn't occurred to him, and it made him a little angry — partly at himself for not thinking of it sooner and partly at Asha for thinking of it so quickly.

"What do you mean?" he cried. "We haven't even opened it!" The squeak in his voice embarrassed him.

"I mean, it might be a gimmick," Asha said. "A trick. Like a toy that flies around in a TV commercial, but then when you get it home and play with it, it just sits there."

Suddenly Oscar felt very heavy, like his heart had slipped down into his shoes. He thought of all the times he'd fallen or tripped or made a fool of himself. Then he thought about gravity, the awful force that pulled him and spun him and caused all of it. He'd been so sure the little bottle would be the solution to all his problems. Now he feared Asha was right.

Tears welled up in Oscar's eyes. He walked out of the caboose and sat down at the top of the steps. He hated crying in front of other people even more than he hated falling or tripping in front of them. He was glad that only Asha was there to see him. He didn't think he could hold back the tears just then even if he'd been standing in front of his whole school.

"Hey," Asha called from inside the caboose.

Oscar didn't answer. After a few minutes, he heard scraping and tapping noises, and he knew Asha was trying to pick the lock.

Maybe that's a good sign, he thought. *Maybe she thinks the gravity repellent will actually work.*

Or maybe she just liked the challenge of getting into a locked case.

Oscar sat on the steps and tried very hard to make the tears stop. He thought about baseball and riding his bike down big hills and ice cream cones and a lot of other things that made him happy. But his thoughts of baseball turned to thoughts of tripping over a base, which turned to thoughts of gravity, which made the tears come back.

Oscar was still sitting there feeling miserable when he heard Asha again. "I did it!" she cried. "I opened it!"

Oscar got up and went back inside the caboose. Asha held up three little bottles triumphantly. "There were two others under the shelf," she explained, grinning. "Maybe there's even more in here somewhere." She looked around curiously.

Oscar half-smiled at her and wiped his eyes with his sleeve.

"Aren't you excited?" she asked.

"It probably doesn't even work," Oscar said, shrugging. "You said so yourself."

"I know. And maybe it won't. But we have it now, so we might as well try it!" Asha said, handing him the bottles.

Oscar reluctantly put two of the bottles into his backpack and stared at the one in his hand.

"Don't be such a pessimist," Asha said, smiling.

"I don't even know what that means," Oscar mumbled, sniffling.

"It means that you don't believe good things ever happen," Asha explained. "But how can you know unless you try?"

~Chapter 9~

Oscar unscrewed the cap and sniffed the contents of the bottle. It didn't smell like anything. He looked at Asha. "Do you think I should drink some?" he asked.

Asha frowned, took the bottle, and read its label very carefully. "I don't know . . ." she said slowly. "What if it's poisonous? You wouldn't drink bug spray."

"True," Oscar said. "So should I put it on my skin?"

Asha considered this for a moment. "Maybe we should test it first," she said, handing the bottle back.

"On what?" Oscar asked, looking around.

"How about the rat in the cupboard?" Asha suggested. "It's dead already, so we can't hurt it."

Oscar shook his head. "No way. I'm not reaching into that cupboard," he said. "Plus, the rat's probably slimy."

"Well, we should test it on *something* first," Asha said. "Let's take it outside."

Oscar carefully screwed the cap back on the bottle and went outside. Asha followed, climbing down the steps after him.

Oscar looked at the big spider, sitting in its web in the corner. "What about him?" he asked, gesturing toward the spider.

"How do you know it's a boy? Didn't you read *Charlotte's Web*?" Asha asked.

"Okay, 'her' then. Should we sprinkle some on her and see what happens?"

Asha looked concerned. "I guess so," she said. But what if it hurts her? Or kills her? We don't know what's in this stuff. Let's try it on something else first."

Oscar thought it was pretty silly to be so concerned about a spider, but that's just how Asha was. "Okay, how about a rock?" he said.

"Perfect," Asha agreed.

Oscar unscrewed the cap and carefully poured a tiny bit of gravity repellent onto a small rock on the ground. When the liquid came out, he half-expected it to sparkle or fizz. But it just looked like plain water coming out of a bottle.

He and Asha held their breath as they watched it. After a few seconds, the rock lifted off the ground and hung, suspended in the air, several inches in front of them. A breeze came through the clearing, and the rock moved along with it, turning gently like an empty grocery bag caught in the wind.

Oscar and Asha turned toward each other, wide-eyed and grinning.

"COOL!" they cried at the same time. They watched the rock float away from them, then looked around for other things they could use to test the repellent.

"*Now* should I put some on the spider?" Oscar asked.

Asha considered this for a moment and looked at the rock. It didn't seem damaged. "Okay," she said slowly. "But just a little bit."

Then Oscar realized there was one *small* problem — he'd have to get close to the spider. "Hmm," he said, leaning back. "Maybe I should paint it on with a piece of grass or something." He looked down at the weeds around his feet.

"Give it to me," Asha said. She took the bottle and approached the web carefully. Then she poured a few drops onto the spider and stepped away.

The kids watched, fascinated, as the spider floated into the air away from her web, attached only by a strand of her silk. Spiders have very small faces, so it can be hard to tell when they're panicked, but Oscar and Asha were fairly sure they were watching a panicked spider. The creature began moving all her legs very quickly and pulling herself down by her own thread of silk. When she reached her web, she hung on tight, curled into a tight spider-ball.

"Aw, poor thing. It scared her," Asha said.

Personally, Oscar felt it was just as well for the spider to cling to her web. It was comforting to realize that gravity affected spiders and other scary things as well. At least it meant he didn't have to worry about one floating toward him out of nowhere.

"She looks okay. I mean, it didn't hurt her or anything, right?" Oscar finally said.

"I guess not," Asha said, shrugging.

"I'm going to put some on myself," Oscar said. He unscrewed the cap and looked at Asha for her reaction.

She raised her eyebrows. "Go for it."

Oscar poured a few drops into the palm of his right hand. After a few moments, his hand felt very light — so light that it floated upward and took his arm with it.

"That's the first time I've ever seen you raise your hand!" Asha giggled.

Oscar bent over and dripped some more of the liquid on his left shoe. This put him into an awkward position, as his left foot floated up in the air just like his right hand had done.

Asha grabbed the bottle as Oscar fell backward and lay on the ground, looking puzzled, as two of his limbs floated in the air above him. He looked as if he were lying in a broken hammock. Oscar giggled at the odd sensations in his right arm and left leg.

Asha watched, fascinated. She thought for a moment, then sprinkled repellent on both of her shoes. She had barely finished screwing the cap back on the bottle when her feet floated out from underneath her and headed straight for the sky. Suddenly she was suspended in the air upside down. Her pigtails hung over her head, and her hands hovered a few inches above the ground.

The two kids looked at each other, Oscar sideways and Asha upside down, and started laughing harder than they'd ever laughed before. They could barely get words out between their giggles.

"Hee hee hee — *gasp* — we should use this stuff — *gasp* — in gym class!" Oscar managed to say.

"A ha ha — *gasp* — hee hee — *gasp* — best handstand ever!" Asha giggled.

"We could — *gasp* — we could climb to the — *gasp* — top of the rope in, like, FIVE SECONDS!" Oscar shouted.

"You could be — hee hee — the champion of square dancing!" Asha yelled.

Oscar stopped laughing and looked at her. "That's not funny," he said. "No one wants to be good at that."

They paused for a moment, then laughed even harder.

Just then, the sunlight broke through the branches of the big tree and shone on both of them. Oscar and Asha were still giggling as they drifted back to the ground.

"Ow!" Asha said, rubbing her head. "What happened?" She picked dried leaves out of her hair.

Oscar felt his left shoe. "I think the repellent dried," he said. "Maybe it only works until it . . . um . . ." He tried to think of the right word.

"Evaporates?" Asha suggested.

"Yeah," Oscar said. He stood up suddenly, grabbing the bottle off the ground. "I'm going to put it all over me."

"Wait," Asha said. "I think we should do that inside somewhere. What if we float away because we don't have anything to hold on to?"

Oscar thought of the panicked spider. He was so excited to use more of the repellent, but he knew Asha was right. He sighed and put the bottle in his backpack. "Okay, let's go."

They were walking away when Asha suddenly stopped and looked back. "Wait a minute," she said, running back to the far end of the caboose.

Oscar heard noises inside and knew Asha was closing the case and putting the lock back in place. Finally she reappeared, rolled the door shut, latched it, and jumped back down to the ground.

She's a great best friend for taking such good care of our treasure, Oscar thought, smiling happily as they headed out of the clearing.

~Chapter 10~

"What should we try first?" Oscar asked. He and Asha sat on the floor of his bedroom, staring at the bottle of gravity repellent between them.

"We should see if we can float in the air. I mean, if our whole bodies can float," Asha said. "I bet if we put enough on and cover ourselves all over, it'll work."

Oscar thought about this and remembered how some of the repellent had dripped out of his hand in the clearing. He had an idea. "We should put it in a spray bottle!" he exclaimed. "That way, we can cover ourselves with it, and we won't waste as much."

"That's an excellent idea," Asha said, smiling. "But where are we going to find an empty spray bottle?"

"We'll just have to find one that's not empty and dump it out," Oscar said. He thought for a moment. "I know where. Come on."

Oscar led Asha into the bathroom he shared with his sister. In her cabinet, Gretchen had dozens of bottles filled with gels, goos, and sprays. Oscar had no idea what she did with them during the hours she locked herself in the bathroom, but with so many to choose from, how could she possibly miss one?

Oscar picked a small spray bottle from the back of the cabinet, unscrewed the cap, and emptied it into the sink. Then he rinsed the bottle out with water and sprayed water through the nozzle several times to clean it. "Ta-da!" he said, handing it to Asha.

Asha carefully poured the repellent into the bottle and screwed the nozzle back on. "Just like bug spray!" She spritzed some on Oscar's foot and smiled.

"Or sunscreen!" Oscar stared as his foot floated into the air. "Spray me all over!" he said.

Asha sprayed his other foot, then both legs. Oscar's lower half floated up into the air so quickly, he did a half-flip and hit his head on the bathroom counter.

"Gurrrf!" he grunted, rubbing his head and clutching the faucet as his legs floated up. "This stuff is supposed to help me *not* run into things!"

"Sorry, Oscar," Asha said. "Maybe I should start with your head and shoulders next time. Here, hold still."

Asha sprayed the repellent on Oscar's stomach and back, and he lurched upward, his arms dangling down. She sprayed his hands and arms next, and they floated up as well. Oscar hung in the air with his head down, like he was looking at something on the bottom of a pool. He turned toward Asha just as she sprayed his head, and some of the repellent went in his mouth.

"Phhhblt!" Oscar sputtered. "Ew! It tastes like dirty socks."

"How do you know what dirty socks taste like?" Asha asked, giggling. She watched him float upward. "How does it feel?"

Oscar's eyes were wide as he floated in the air between the bathroom lights and the shower curtain. "It feels . . ." he began, "it feels like . . . the weirdest thing ever." He waved his arms gently back and forth. "Nothing's pulling on me." He smiled down at Asha.

Asha looked around at the objects in the bathroom. "Hey, try something," she said.

"Like what?" Oscar asked. He made swimming motions with his hands to see if he could pull himself forward.

"Grab the shower curtain rod, and push off from it to spin yourself."

Oscar grabbed it. "Push off how?" he asked.

"Pretend you're in your dad's office chair and the rod is his desk," Asha told him.

Oscar smiled. When he was younger, one of his favorite things to do had been to spin around in his dad's office chair. Now he grabbed the rod and pushed off it — hard. He spun fast in the other direction, like a roll of toilet paper unraveling.

"Wow!" Asha exclaimed.

Oscar laughed and shrieked as he turned around and around and around. He saw Asha, mirror, ceiling, shower rod, Asha, mirror, ceiling, shower rod.

Finally his spinning slowed, and Oscar began to drift toward the floor. "That was fun!" he cried. "Spray me again!"

"No, it's my turn!" Asha said. "You spray me now."

"Okay, okay," Oscar said as he pulled himself down and put his feet on the floor. "You have to try spinning. That was a great idea." He leaned down to spray Asha's feet.

"Top first, remember?" she said.

"Okay, but close your mouth. It tastes really nasty."

Asha shut her eyes and mouth, and Oscar sprayed her evenly from head to toe. She floated up so quickly that she had to put her hands on the ceiling so she wouldn't bump her head.

"Wow!" she cried. "This feels so weird!"

"Try the spinning thing!" Oscar said.

Asha pulled herself over to the shower rod and pushed against it. She spun around a few times, then grabbed the rod to stop herself. "Ugh. That makes me feel like puking."

As Asha faced the mirror and turned herself upside down, Oscar sprayed more gravity repellent on himself and floated up next to her. They stared at their reflections.

"We look like astronauts," Asha said. "Remember that video of the moonwalk Mrs. Faust showed us?"

"I'll race you back to the space station," Oscar said.

Giggling, they pushed and pulled to get past each other, swimming out into the hallway and into Oscar's bedroom.

"Wow, my room looks so different from up here," Oscar said as he floated a few inches from the ceiling and gazed down at everything from above. He saw dust on the top of his bookcase and a couple of toys that had fallen behind his dresser.

So that's where Jar-Jar Binks went, Oscar thought to himself.

Just then, Asha gave him a push from behind, sending them flying in opposite directions. She laughed as he bounced gently off a wall. "You're a human pinball!" she cried.

"Poing . . . poing, puh-poing!" Oscar shouted as he curled up in a ball and bounced from one wall to the other. His sneakers left gray waffle-pattern shoe prints high on the wall.

"Uh-oh," Asha said, watching. "Those will be hard to explain."

Oscar shrugged. He wasn't concerned. His parents were used to seeing odd messes in the house. They didn't ask him a lot of questions about it as long as he cleaned up after himself. They knew he didn't mean to be so klutzy.

"Hey, watch this!" Asha said. She raised her arms above her head and swung them down to her sides quickly. She curled into a ball and spun forward in a midair somersault. Then she pushed her arms back out to slow down, knocking some of Oscar's action figures off the top shelf of his bookcase in the process.

"Careful, Asha!" Oscar cried. "Those are my favorite ones."

"Sorry!"

They stopped spinning and bouncing and looked at each other. Asha had never been klutzy before, and Oscar had never said the word "careful" to someone else. They both laughed at how upside down their world had become — literally.

Just then, Oscar heard a car pull up outside. "My mom's home!" he said. "Close the door!"

Asha pulled herself over to the door, grabbed the top corner, and pushed it shut. "We've got to dry off and get down!" she cried frantically. "Swing your arms and legs around — fast!"

They both started waving their hands back and forth like they did in the school bathroom when the paper towels ran out. Oscar pushed his legs around and around, pedaling an invisible bicycle. Asha blew on her T-shirt and kicked her legs like she'd learned in swim class.

They were so preoccupied with drying themselves off that they didn't even notice their motions were having an effect. Oscar turned upside down, and Asha drifted toward him. Her head collided with his knees, which were still moving up and down rapidly.

"Ow ow ow!" Asha cried as he kicked her.

"Sorry!" Oscar said.

"Oscar, are you in there?" his mother called.

Asha and Oscar looked at each other, panicked.

"Um, yeah, I'm here!" Oscar yelled. "I'll be out in a second!"

Asha finished drying off and drifted down to the floor. She grabbed Oscar and turned him right side up. He grabbed the back of his desk chair and pulled himself down to the floor, yanking a heavy box of Legos onto his lap to weigh himself down just as his mother opened the door.

"Oh, hi, Asha," his mother said with a smile. She held a package out to her son. "Oscar, I bought you a dress shirt for that party we're going to on Saturday. Can you try it on for me to see if it fits?"

"Right now?" Oscar asked, hoping his mother couldn't hear how loudly his heart was beating. He knew if he took the box off his lap, he might go flying upward. Oscar didn't know what his parents would do if they found out about Dr. Oopsie's repellent, and he didn't want to find out. He took the package and began opening it very slowly to buy himself some time.

Asha sensed his dilemma and stood up. "Whose party is it, Mrs. Schmidt?" she asked politely.

While Asha had an impressively grown-up conversation with his mother, Oscar felt his sweatshirt and pants to make sure they were dry. When he was certain he wouldn't start floating again, he pulled the box out of his lap and stood up.

"Sweetie, what *happened* to you?" his mother cried when she saw him from head to toe. "Did you hurt yourself?" She inspected his skinned chin, dirty sweatshirt, and ripped pants.

"A little, but I'm okay," Oscar mumbled.

His mother pulled him toward her and held his face in her hands, which embarrassed him in front of Asha. "My accident-prone little prince," she said fondly, kissing him on the forehead.

"MO-OM!" Oscar cried, trying to pull away from her.

Asha tried not to smile. "I should go home," she said. "It's almost dinnertime. Bye, Mrs. Schmidt. See you tomorrow, Oscar!"

"Bye, Asha," Oscar's mom said as she fussed over his dirty sweatshirt.

Asha ran into the bathroom and grabbed the gravity repellent. She came back to the door of Oscar's bedroom and showed the bottle to him over his mother's shoulder. Then she winked and put it back in her pocket so he knew it was safe.

～Chapter 11～

That night after dinner, Oscar stashed the other two bottles of gravity repellent safely in his dresser and made a list of things he wanted to do with it. There were only three small bottles total, and they had already used about one-fifth of the bottle Asha had taken home with her.

We should return to the caboose as soon as possible, Oscar thought, *to see if there's any more.*

In the meantime, he needed to come up with a plan. Oscar thought for a long time about what he most wanted to do. He wrote:

#1 FLY

#2 BUILD TREE HOUSE IN TOP OF TREE

#3 CLIMB ROPE IN GYM CLASS

#4 MAKE TOYS FLY AROUND ROOM

#5 MAKE GRETCHEN FLY AROUND ROOM

He thought about the last one for a minute. Then he changed it to:

#5 MAKE GRETCHEN'S PHONE FLY AROUND ROOM

Oscar chewed on the end of his pen and tried to think of other things. He thought back to the excitement he'd felt when he'd first found the gravity repellent. What had he wanted to do more than anything else? He added:

#6 WALK WITHOUT TRIPPING OR FALLING

He thought about it more and wrote:

#7 RUN WITHOUT TRIPPING OR FALLING

And finally:

#8 PLAY BASEBALL WITHOUT TRIPPING OR FALLING

Oscar realized he would need *a lot* more repellent to make himself less klutzy. Or he'd have to give up using the repellent for fun and use a tiny bit every day when he needed it. But there was no way he would give up the stuff at the top of his list.

Oscar lay awake in bed that night, staring at his shoeprints on the ceiling and wall and wondering how much repellent he'd need to walk without tripping. He didn't need to float, but maybe he could be a tiny bit lighter. Then the earth wouldn't pull on him quite so much.

It sounds like a dream, Oscar thought as he yawned and drifted off to sleep.

* * *

When Oscar met Asha in front of her house the next morning, she wasn't carrying the spray bottle. "Where's the repellent?" he asked.

"I thought about it, and I don't think we should bring it to school," Asha answered. "What if someone takes it?"

Oscar thought about the bully and his friends, but he also thought about his list. "But how can we use it in gym class if we leave it at home?"

Asha frowned. "If we float up to the ceiling in gym, Ms. Parker will definitely find out about it," she said. "Then we'll end up in the principal's office. Who knows what might happen then?"

She had a point, but Oscar was disappointed that he wouldn't get to show off in front of his classmates. The day had just started, and he already had to scratch something off his list.

"Okay, fine," he said with a sigh. "But I want to try something. Will you go get the repellent?"

"But . . ." Asha started to say.

"I don't want to take it with us, I just want to use a little bit now," Oscar explained.

Asha went back in her house and returned a moment later, carrying the small spray bottle.

"Spray a tiny, tiny bit on my stomach and back," Oscar said. He held up his arms and turned in a circle as she sprayed. "Now watch."

Oscar turned and walked to the end of the block. He dared himself to look up rather than down like he normally would. After a dozen steps, Oscar turned around and walked back toward Asha. He didn't trip once. When he reached her, he smiled and raised his arms over his head like he saw athletes do in the Olympics.

"Bravo!" Asha cried.

Asha took the bottle back inside, and she and Oscar walked to school. He didn't trip or fall once, and he felt taller as he walked past the nurse's office. The nurse glanced up, ready to clean a scrape or unwrap a Band-Aid for him. She smiled at him as he went by.

During class, Oscar passed his list to Asha. She read it, smiled, added something, and passed it back. Now the bottom of the note said:

#9 Find your lost Frisbee on the roof

Oscar nodded. He chewed on the end of his pencil and stared out the window. Some fifth graders were outside playing tetherball. Oscar watched the rope coil around the pole as the ball flew faster and faster. His eyes widened, and he wrote:

#10 RIDE SEALING FAN

Oscar passed the note back to Asha, who studied it with a confused look on her face. Then she crossed out something, wrote something next to it, and handed the list back to Oscar, who quickly hid it in his lap as Mrs. Faust looked in his direction. When the teacher turned back toward the chalkboard, he looked at what Asha had written:

#10 RIDE SEALING FAN Ride ceiling fan (But what if we break it?)

Oscar frowned and wrote back:

YOUR NO FUN

They passed the note back and forth:

YOUR NO FUN You're no fun.

If it breaks, how would we explain to your parents?

WE WON'T BREAK IT

We might.

IT'S STRONG

How do you know?

TIED BUZZ LIGHTYEAR TO IT BEFORE AND IT WAS OKAY

Okay, but I don't think it's a great idea.

YOU WORRY TOO MUCH

~Chapter 12~

After school that day, Oscar and Asha stood in the center of his living room, staring up at the ceiling fan. Gretchen was at home as usual. On weekdays, she was supposed to keep an eye on Oscar until their parents got home from work. But she rarely left her room, where she sat on her bed with her laptop and phone all afternoon.

While Oscar and Asha talked about their ceiling-fan plan, Gretchen sang along to the music in her earbuds. Oscar knew he could set the house on fire, and Gretchen would only look up when the firefighters turned the hose on her.

"I don't know, Oscar . . ." Asha said, shaking her head. She watched the blades of the fan turn around and around. "I don't want to get in trouble with your parents if we break it."

"I'm telling you, it'll be fine," Oscar insisted. "We'll be weightless, remember? It would only break if we actually pulled on it."

Asha narrowed her eyes, and Oscar could tell she was working something out in her head.

"I think it'll be okay . . ." she finally said. "If we hold on to it on opposite sides."

"Of course we will," Oscar said. "If we didn't, we'd be in each others' way."

Asha was lost in her thoughts and didn't seem to hear him. "We need to balance the weight, so that the —"

"Geez, you sound like my parents," Oscar interrupted impatiently. "We're pretty sure it'll work, so let's just try it." He picked up the bottle of gravity repellent and sprayed his head and shoulders. He moved on to his lower body, and as he floated upward he tossed the bottle down to Asha.

Once Oscar was at eye level with the ceiling fan, he realized its blades seemed to be turning awfully fast. "You know," he began, "maybe we should start at the lowest speed. Just to . . . see how it is first."

Asha went over to the wall and switched the fan speed to low. Oscar breathed a silent sigh of relief as the blades slowed down. Then she sprayed herself all over and quickly placed the bottle on the coffee table as she floated upward. The two hung in the air on opposite sides of the fan, their heads level with the blades.

"I think we should grab on at the same time," Asha said. "Otherwise we might break it."

Oscar didn't move. Riding the ceiling fan sounded much more fun when he imagined it earlier. But now that the blades were whipping past right in front of his face, his heart beat loudly in his ears.

"Are you ready to grab on?" Asha asked.

Oscar didn't say anything; he just stared at the blades whizzing by. His eyes followed one and then the next, back and forth.

"Oscar?" Asha said.

Oscar shook his head to clear the nervous thoughts and tried not to listen to his heartbeat. "I'm ready."

"On three, we'll each grab the blade that's closest to us, okay?" Asha said.

Oscar nodded.

"One . . ." Asha counted.

Oscar brought his hands up near his ears.

"Two . . ."

Oscar tensed and rubbed his fingers together like a thief in a movie getting ready to steal something.

"Three!" Asha exclaimed.

Oscar closed his hands over the blade coming toward him and shut his eyes tightly. The fan slowed for a moment, and then he felt himself being pulled through the air. When Oscar opened his eyes, he saw Asha smiling on the other side.

"Whee!" Asha cried as her legs floated out behind her.

Riding the fan felt a little like the merry-go-round on the school playground, but something was different. When Oscar let go of the bar on the merry-go-round, he could never balance like some of the other kids did. He always got dumped off the edge onto the gravel.

But now, wearing the gravity repellent, Oscar felt like he was flying. His smile stretched so wide, he thought it would touch his ears. The weightless motion felt so wonderful that he didn't hear Asha calling his name.

"Oscar!" she said again, more loudly.

"What?" Oscar said. He looked up at Asha and saw the walls rushing by behind her head.

"I'm drying off," she said. "I have to let go."

"Okay," he said. "Go ahead."

"You have to let go at the same time," she said. "Remember? Otherwise we might break the fan."

"I don't want to!" Oscar cried. "This is fun!"

"Oscar, let go!"

"No. It'll be fine. Just let go yourself!" he shouted.

"You're going to break it!" Asha said, her legs beginning to dip behind her.

Oscar felt his own legs begin to drift downwards, and the familiar pulling sensation from the merry-go-round returned. The gravity repellent was wearing off. "Okay, fine," he said reluctantly. "I'm letting go now."

Oscar and Asha both let go of their fan blades at the same time and floated off in opposite directions. Asha knocked over a lamp as she bounced gently off a wall and landed upside down on the couch.

The motion of the fan sent Oscar into the kitchen, where he bounced once on the countertop island in the middle of the room. He landed on a stack of junk mail, slid along the counter, and fell over the far side onto the floor. His arm caught a bowl of fruit and toppled it, sending apples and oranges rolling off the counter and onto his head. Oscar remembered Isaac Newton sitting under the tree, and he began to giggle.

"Are you okay?" Asha called from the other room.

His giggle became a guffaw, and soon Oscar was laughing so hard he couldn't answer her. He held his stomach as he lay on the kitchen floor. He laughed and snorted as happy tears rolled out of the corners of his eyes into his ears. This tickled his ears and made him laugh even harder.

Asha stood the lamp upright and came into the kitchen. She saw Oscar on the floor, surrounded by spilled junk mail and bruised fruit, and started to giggle too. She sat down next to him and piled the papers, apples, and oranges on top of him. They both giggled and guffawed until their sides hurt.

"That was the best thing ever!" Asha said, still laughing.

"I felt like Superman!" Oscar cried, pointing his arms out in front of him.

"You *looked* like Superman — at least until you flew into the kitchen and made a mess," Asha said, smiling.

After a minute or two, Oscar sat up. He pushed the papers and fruit out of his lap and pulled the list out of his pocket. Using a pen he found in the pile of junk mail, he crossed off an item:

~~#10 Ride ceiling fan~~

Oscar scanned the rest of the list and looked up at Asha with a mischievous grin. "Let's fly for real," he said.

* * *

Several minutes later, Asha stood over Oscar as he pulled things out of his bedroom closet. "I don't think this is a good idea," she said.

"Why not?" Oscar asked. He found his binoculars and stuffed them into his backpack.

"Someone might see you," she said.

"I don't care," Oscar said, shrugging. He was too excited to worry about that. He added a double knot to his shoelaces, put on the backpack, and went out to his front yard.

"I don't believe that you don't care," Asha said as she followed him outside.

Oscar pretended not to hear that, so she stood right in front of him so he couldn't look past her.

"It's not safe," she said. "You don't know how high you'll go."

"That's the whole point!" Oscar said, gazing up at the sky. "I want to fly outside, not just around the living room."

"What happens when you dry off?" Asha asked. "You might fall really fast."

Oscar squinted at the light clouds covering the sun. "It's not that hot out," he said. "I'll dry off slowly and drift down." He took the bottle of repellent out of the backpack and aimed the nozzle at his head.

"What if you run into something?" Asha asked.

"There's nothing to run into," Oscar said as he gestured at the sky. "That's why they call it air instead of ground."

"What about those?" Asha asked, pointing to the power lines that ran behind the houses.

"What about them?" Oscar asked.

"Haven't you ever seen *Jurassic Park*?" Asha cried. "The kid is holding on to the power lines, and then they get turned on and he goes flying! I don't want you to turn into human toast."

Oscar stared at the power lines and remembered the rock moving with the breeze in the clearing. He didn't want to turn into human toast either. But the thought of flying for real thrilled him so much, it was hard to resist.

As he was thinking, Asha grabbed the repellent out of his hand.

"Hey!" Oscar cried. "Give that back!"

"Not until you stop being dumb," she said.

"I'm not being dumb; you're being bossy!" Oscar shouted, grabbing the repellent.

"I'm trying to keep you from hurting yourself!" Asha said.

"You're trying to keep me from having any fun!" Oscar insisted.

They both scrambled to hold on to the bottle, twisting and turning to reach for it. Oscar pulled it out of Asha's hands. Asha grabbed it back, put it on the ground, and sat on it.

"AA-SHAA!" Oscar yelled. He didn't like arguing with her, so he slumped down on the ground and picked at the grass. He knew she was right about some of it, but he also thought she was being way too careful.

Oscar took a deep breath before he spoke. "Why are you being such a pessimist?" he said, reminding her of what she had said the day before. "What do you think is going to happen?"

Asha counted things on her fingers as she said them. "You could run into a power line. You could fly too high and dry off too fast. You could land on a high roof that you can't get down from. You could run into a helicopter —"

"Oh, come on," Oscar interrupted. "A helicopter?"

"Okay, fine. That probably wouldn't happen, but the rest might." Asha thought for another moment. "You said you wouldn't care if someone saw you, but *think* about it."

Oscar stopped picking at the grass. *She's right*, he thought. If other people saw him floating, they'd certainly ask questions. They might even report it to someone, especially if they thought he was in danger. If the police or the fire department got involved, Oscar would *have* to tell them about the repellent. And he wasn't ready to share the secret with anyone but Asha. He pouted and picked at the grass again.

"Hey," Asha said.

Oscar didn't look up.

"Hey!" Asha said again, and nudged him with her elbow.

"What?" Oscar muttered.

"What else does it say on your list?" she asked.

"Number one is *fly*," he said, glaring at her.

"What's number two?" Asha asked cheerfully, ignoring his glare.

Oscar pulled the list out of his pocket and looked at it. "Build a tree house in the top of the tree," he said with a sigh.

"The huge one in your backyard?" Asha asked.

Oscar nodded without much enthusiasm.

Asha stood up, brushed off her shorts, and tossed the bottle of gravity repellent in Oscar's lap. "So let's go climb to the top of it," she said.

⌒Chapter 13⌒

The tree in Oscar's backyard was enormous. He and Asha had never seen the top of it. Even from the second-floor windows in his house, they could only see the middle of the tree. In the summer, the branches got so thick with leaves that the trunk seemed to disappear halfway up.

They had long thought that it would be a perfect place for a tree house, but they couldn't figure out how to get *into* the tree to build it. The lower part of its trunk was too smooth, with hardly any handholds or footholds to grab for climbing.

Oscar had longed to climb the tree ever since his fifth birthday party when he let go of a balloon and it had floated up away from him. One moment he'd been holding it, and a few moments later the wind had carried it up and around the tree. Oscar had run to the corner of the yard to see past the tree, expecting the balloon to appear again, higher in the sky. But it never did. It hadn't occurred to him that something could just vanish into a tree.

There must be a secret space up there, Oscar had thought, *a space where I could hide too.*

But even if he could climb the tree, Oscar wasn't allowed anywhere near it. Every time he asked his parents if he could nail some wooden pieces to its trunk so he could climb it, the answer was absolutely not.

"You'll break your neck!" his mother and father always said.

Oscar didn't understand what the big deal was. His neck was such a small part of his body. He'd broken half a dozen bones before. His neck wasn't even a fun, useful part like a foot or an elbow.

Today, even though he knew he wasn't supposed to, Oscar couldn't resist climbing it.

The tree itself isn't dangerous, he reasoned. *Gravity is.*

Standing at the base of the tree, Oscar was so excited that he forgot to be disappointed about not flying. He quickly sprayed himself all over with repellent and tossed the bottle to Asha as he floated up the tree's trunk. He grabbed the first branch he could reach, wrapped his legs around it, and swung upside down.

"Woo-HOO!" he shouted.

"Shhhh!" Asha whispered loudly from the ground. "Keep it down! You want to advertise it to the whole neighborhood?"

Oscar clapped a hand over his mouth. It was hard to keep quiet when he was having so much fun.

Asha sprayed the repellent all over her body, then stuffed the bottle in a pocket of her shorts as she floated up the trunk and into the cover of the leafy branches. It was remarkably cool and dark in the space around the trunk, and it smelled fresh and green, like the shop where Oscar's mother sometimes bought flowers.

They pulled themselves up through the branches, amazed at how easy it was without gravity pulling them down. Oscar had often watched squirrels race up the side of the tree and hop easily among the lower branches. Now he had the distinct sense of being a squirrel, so light that the branches hardly bent as he pulled on them.

Inside the leaf cover it looked like a different world — a place where all kinds of things happened that were invisible from the outside. They saw a small bird's nest in a corner where one branch grew out of another. It appeared empty at first, but when they looked closer, they saw fluffy bits of feathers and pieces of light-blue eggshell. Higher up, they found a hollow filled with acorns and other bits of food.

"Hey, that's the crust I dropped yesterday morning!" Asha exclaimed, pointing. She'd been running late to school and had left her house with a piece of peanut butter toast. She didn't like crusts, so she had dropped it into a bush next to the sidewalk. Apparently the squirrel that lived in this hollow enjoyed crusts more than Asha did.

Oscar envied the squirrel and the birds — the tree seemed like a fantastic place to live. It was so quiet, and it felt safe and protected thanks to the leaf cover. He and Asha continued to pull themselves up through the branches until they found two spots where they could sit comfortably.

Oscar and Asha nestled into the chair-branches, hooking their feet under them so they wouldn't float away. They looked at each other and giggled. The caboose was the coolest tree house ever, but this was a close second.

Just then, a breeze came through the branches and parted some of the leaves in front of them.

"WHOAAA!" they exclaimed at the same time. From where they sat, they could see over the tops of all the houses on their block. Now they knew how tall the tree really was.

TINA L. PETERSON

"My Frisbee!" Oscar exclaimed, pointing at a red disc on the roof of Asha's house. "We have to remember to get that down."

"Look, someone lost his swim trunks," Asha said when the breeze parted the leaves again. She pointed to a brightly colored pair of shorts on a roof across the street. "How did they get up there?"

The sun came out from behind one cloud and disappeared behind another. For a brief moment, the light sparkled off something behind Asha. Oscar peered at it. Hanging from a branch was a limp piece of red rubber tied with a silver ribbon. It was the balloon from his birthday party! He couldn't believe it was still there.

"Asha, look!" Oscar said, pointing.

She turned around. "What is it?"

"The balloon I lost on my birthday when I was five!" he said. "Can you reach it?"

139

Asha looked at it, turned back to Oscar, and made a face. "Why do you want an old deflated balloon?"

"I just do," Oscar said. "Can you try to grab it? Please?"

Asha shrugged and unhooked her legs from the tree trunk. Then she pulled herself along the branch until her feet stuck out from inside the leaf cover. She grabbed the balloon and began to unwind the silver ribbon from the branch.

Just then, the sun came out from behind the clouds altogether. Sunlight streamed through the leaves onto Asha, and she yelped as her legs began to float downward. She turned onto her stomach to grab on to the branch, which was bending slowly underneath her. "I'm drying off!" Asha cried, her eyes wide with panic. "Help!"

Oscar realized in horror that the bottle of gravity repellent was in the pocket of Asha's shorts. There was no time to float down and get it out. She would get too heavy too quickly.

Oscar pulled himself down to where Asha hung and grabbed her arms. He wrapped his legs around the nearest branch and held on as she grew heavier and heavier. Oscar's hands began to sweat, and he heard a branch snap as Asha slipped out of his grip.

"OSCAAAAR!"

~Chapter 14~

I must have closed my eyes, Oscar thought. He hadn't seen Asha fall, and he barely remembered racing down the tree trunk to help her. But he could recall being in the ambulance and then the hospital. And he remembered crying, which embarrassed him.

Now he sat in a hospital waiting room with Gretchen and Asha's father. He was so terrified he couldn't speak. Everyone seemed to get that, because they didn't ask him many questions.

It's all my fault, Oscar thought. *Asha never would have played with the repellent unless I shared it with her. And she never would have fallen out of the tree if I hadn't asked her to reach for my old balloon. It should have been me. Stupid gravity repellent. Stupid me.*

It had only been a few hours ago that Asha had stopped him from floating off into power lines. She'd wanted to protect him, to keep him from being careless.

Oscar began to cry again. He didn't care who saw him anymore. Gretchen looked at him and put her arm around his shoulders. Her phone was in her pocket, but she hadn't taken it out once since they got to the hospital.

Just then, a doctor in a white coat came out into the waiting room. "Mr. Banerjee?" she asked.

Asha's father stood up. "Yes, that's me. Please tell me, how is she?"

"She's fine, sir," the doctor said. "A broken leg, but it should heal quickly. She's a little shaken up, of course, but she'll be able to go home tonight."

When he heard the word *fine*, Oscar's heart leaped up into his throat. His best friend in the world would be okay.

Asha's father seemed to sag with relief. "Thank you, Doctor. Thank you so much. Can I go back and see her?"

"Of course," the doctor replied. "Please come with me."

Mr. Banerjee turned to Gretchen and Oscar. "Let me go in and see her first," he said. "Then I'll come for you two. Okay?"

Gretchen and Oscar nodded silently. Oscar let out the breath he'd been holding and suddenly felt light-headed and dizzy. He noticed that Gretchen looked worried, and it suddenly occurred to him that she might get in trouble too. After all, she was supposed to have been watching them that afternoon.

As if on cue, Gretchen turned to him. "How did you get up the tree?" she asked. "There's nothing on the trunk to hold on to."

Oscar tried to look calm as he thought about how to answer. He certainly didn't want Gretchen to know about the repellent. If he said they'd used a rope, she would ask more questions and maybe even check the tree when they got home. There was only one solution — he decided to tell her one thing that was true, and to tell her more about it than she ever wanted to know.

"Oh, it was really hard," Oscar began. "But we've been doing, um . . . rock climbing in gym class. We've learned about all these different kinds of, um . . . handholds you can use. There's this one called a pinch that you can use on knobs sticking out of the tree. And we tried another one called a . . . a sidepull, and that worked really well on the tree bark. When you use it, it's like you . . ."

Oscar went on like this for some time. He was amazed at how convincing he sounded. As he talked, he almost believed it himself. But the important thing was that it convinced Gretchen, who began to look bored almost immediately. He knew she wouldn't ask any more questions, and she certainly wouldn't want a demonstration.

After some time, Mr. Banerjee came back out to the waiting room and motioned to them. Oscar and Gretchen stood up and followed him down the hall to Asha's room. Oscar had expected his friend to have tubes sticking out every which way, but she looked more or less like she had that afternoon, except that now she was wearing a blue nightgown.

When he and Gretchen entered the room, Asha was sitting up in bed and talking on the phone to her mother, who was out of town on a business trip. Oscar realized with a start that Asha might have told her parents about the repellent. His eyes grew wide, and he stood frozen, waiting for her to say something.

"I'm fine, Ma," Asha said into the phone. "We were rock climbing . . . no, on a tree. The big one in Oscar's backyard . . . no, it doesn't hurt . . . "

As he listened to her talk to her mother, Oscar's heart nearly leaped out of his chest. He couldn't believe that they'd thought of the same exact story to tell. *Did Asha read my mind*, he wondered, *or did I read hers?* Either way, it made him incredibly happy. He wanted to hug her, but she looked so delicate lying in the hospital bed.

Asha said goodbye to her mother and handed the phone back to her father. "Check it out," she said to Oscar. She pulled away a blanket covering her legs. Her whole left leg, from her midthigh down to the start of her toes, was encased in a pink cast.

Oscar had broken many bones, so he was used to casts. Whenever he got one on his left arm, or either leg, or anything that wasn't his right hand, he drew all over it. But he'd never had one this big before. It looked like a giant coloring book.

Oscar put his hands on the cast and started to trace shapes with his fingers. "I have a brand-new pack of markers at home," he said excitedly, "We can design tattoos, and color it, and —"

"Maybe a bit later, okay?" Mr. Banerjee interrupted, putting his hand on Oscar's shoulder. "Asha needs to rest. You two are very lucky that only this happened. It could have been a lot worse."

Oscar felt terrible all over again. He stepped back and swallowed hard to keep from crying for the third time that day. *I might set some kind of world record if I keep this up*, he thought.

Just then Oscar's parents came into the room carrying a stuffed bear dressed as a nurse. His dad handed the bear to Asha, while his mom hugged Oscar and kissed Asha on the forehead. Usually Oscar didn't like it when his mom hugged him in front of other people, but the smell of her coat comforted him after the long, scary day.

Gretchen and the grown-ups stood around for a while talking about the accident. His sister repeated the story Oscar had told her, which matched Asha's story pretty closely. Oscar knew he would be in some trouble when they got home, but fortunately, he'd broken enough bones that his parents tended to be pretty calm about such accidents.

While the grown-ups talked and Gretchen went back to tapping on her phone, Oscar stood next to Asha and smiled awkwardly. He wanted to tell her how scared he'd been and how sorry he was that he'd asked her to reach for the balloon. But if he said all that, he was sure he'd start crying again, and he was tired of the lump in his throat. "I'm really glad you're okay," he said instead, smiling.

Asha smiled back, and Oscar knew she understood everything else he wanted to say.

Oscar looked down and played with the edge of the hospital blanket for a moment. "Maybe we should leave gravity alone for a while," he whispered.

Asha nodded. "That's probably a good idea. But I bet Dr. Oopsie has tons of other cool stuff," she whispered back, smiling.

~Chapter 15~

Only five days had passed since Asha had fallen out of the tree, but Oscar could tell she was already getting sick of her cast. She complained that it made her walk really slowly, and that the crutches hurt her armpits. She had to use a wooden ruler to reach inside the cast and scratch her leg, which she said itched terribly.

The tattoo designs Oscar had drawn all over it didn't seem to help either. It was still a big, heavy piece of plaster that Asha had to drag everywhere, and Oscar felt terrible as he watched her struggle with it. He tried to help by spraying the cast with gravity repellent to make it easier for her to walk. But if he used too much, the cast started to float like a big, ugly balloon.

Because of all this, Asha was pretty grumpy. Her father drove her to and from school while she had the cast, and when she got home she wanted to stay in her room most of the time. And despite what she'd said at the hospital, she didn't mention going back to explore Dr. Oopsie's caboose again.

Oscar missed his friend and was worried she'd lost interest, but he couldn't do anything about it. His parents had grounded him after the tree incident. He wasn't allowed to watch TV or get on the Internet for a week, and he had to come straight home after school.

This last part didn't make much sense to him, because the accident had happened while he was at home. *If they don't want it to happen again, they should make me stay out all afternoon*, Oscar thought.

One day after school, as he watched Asha wrestle her cast into her dad's car, Oscar began to worry about the caboose. He hadn't visited it in almost a week. What if the vines had slipped and someone else had seen it? Oscar decided to take a quick detour to the clearing on his way home from school, just long enough to make sure the train car was still hidden.

Oscar walked quickly to where he usually saw the raccoon. It was easy to find this time, and he was proud that he'd remembered it. As he approached the spot with the Dumpster, Oscar heard laughter and shouting. Then he heard voices. One of them was so familiar that it made the hair on the back of Oscar's neck stand up.

Peering around the corner, Oscar saw Zach and his friends sitting on overturned cardboard boxes, eating chips and drinking soda.

Oscar tried to slow the beating of his heart as he listened to them. *How can I get past without being noticed?* he wondered. If they saw him disappear into the bushes, they might follow him and find the caboose themselves. That was a risk he couldn't take.

PWANG! A loud noise made Oscar jump. He peered at the boys and saw them throwing their empty soda cans at the outside of the Dumpster.

Clearly startled, the raccoon scurried out from underneath, its black-masked eyes wider than Oscar had ever seen them. The boys hooted, picked up the soda cans, and threw them at the animal as it ran into the bushes.

Oscar watched them, furious and panicked. How could they be so mean to the raccoon? He was relieved when he saw the animal disappear inside the pipe, but he was also worried. *What if Zach and the other boys followed it?* he thought. He watched the boys for a few minutes, but they didn't seem interested in the raccoon once they couldn't throw things at it anymore.

Knowing the bully and his friends were so close to his treasure terrified Oscar. But he couldn't do anything about it until the end of the week when he was no longer grounded. Holding his breath and trying to be as quiet as possible, Oscar backed slowly away and went home.

Oscar spent the rest of the afternoon lying on his bed staring at the ceiling. He tried not to think about what Zach and his friends might do to the caboose if they ever found it.

* * *

A few days later, Oscar's parents finally ungrounded him. He immediately went next door to see Asha. Even though she said she didn't feel like leaving her room, he knew she had to be getting bored in there.

Because the accident had been his fault, Oscar felt like it was his job to keep Asha company while she recovered. He also wanted to persuade her to return to the caboose with him as soon as possible. He was worried about leaving it alone for so long.

When Oscar arrived, he found Asha lying on her bed, surrounded by books. "Where did all these come from?" he asked, picking one up and looking at it.

"Library," Asha replied, not looking up. "My parents have gone back to get more three times already."

"Huh. That's a lot of books. Do you know even more big words now?" Oscar teased her, smiling.

Asha rolled her eyes.

"Hey, how about we go explore the caboose again?" Oscar suggested. "I can help you walk."

"I don't feel like it," Asha said with a sigh. "My leg itches like crazy, and this cast is really heavy." She picked up another book and sank farther into the pillows on her bed.

Oscar looked around, trying to think of something he could do to cheer her up or at least make her laugh. He spotted a bowl of loose beads on her desk and grabbed a handful. He took the gravity repellent out of his pocket and sprayed some on the beads in his hand.

"Hey, watch!" Oscar said. He tossed the beads into the air in several different directions, and they floated around the room, bouncing off the walls. It looked really cool until they dried off and fell to the ground, scattering among toys and stuffed animals. Asha looked up from her book but then went back to reading.

Next Oscar grabbed a Barbie doll and a Ken doll and sprayed them. He also sprayed an oddly shaped structure made of Legos and floated the dolls around it like astronauts at a space station. Oscar cupped his hand over his mouth and imitated their voices and the static on walkie-talkies.

"Barbie . . . *kshhh* . . . there's a hole in the solar panel. *Kshhh* . . . do you copy?"

"*Kshhh* . . . copy that, Ken. Can you fix it?"

"Negative, Barbie . . . *kshhh* . . . not without some prechewed bubble gum . . . *kshhh* . . . do you copy?"

"Copy that, Ken. Prechewed bubble gum is on its way. Barbie over and out . . . *kshhh*."

Asha tried hard not to smile.

Oscar rummaged in Asha's closet and found a frilly pink dress. He sprayed the top and made it float in front of him. Then he took a headband from the top of her dresser and placed it on top of his head like a crown. He waved Asha's leg-scratching ruler around like a magic wand and tapped her on the head with it. Asha looked up and smiled at the sight of Oscar with the dress and headband.

"I'm your fairy godmother, Asha-rella," Oscar said in a high-pitched voice. "What is your wish?"

Just then, the still-floating Barbie doll drifted toward Oscar's head and poked him in the eye with one of her pointed toes. "Ow," Oscar said, pushing the doll away.

Asha giggled at this in spite of herself.

Oscar raised the ruler again and got back into character. "Don't you wish to visit the caboose once more?" he squeaked. "Don't you wish to see what other *magical* things await you inside? I can help you get there with my *magical* powers!" Oscar twirled the ruler in circles over her cast.

Asha put her book down at last. She seemed to be warming to the idea. "I don't know . . . I don't think my mom wants me to go very far from the house."

"Tell her . . ." Oscar said, scratching his head, "tell her you want to go to the library because . . . you finished all these books, and you want to pick out some yourself. Parents never say no to more books — especially yours."

Asha nodded. "Okay," she agreed. "But then I should *actually* go to the library."

"We'll stop there on our way back," Oscar assured her.

Asha pulled herself off the bed, got her crutches, and went to ask her mother's permission to go to the library. When she came back she was grinning. The thought of exploring the caboose again seemed to have cheered her up. The endless possibilities hidden inside were too much for anyone to resist.

~Chapter 16~

Oscar thought hard about how to help Asha walk more comfortably. He sprayed a tiny bit of repellent under her arms, so gravity wouldn't pull them down so hard against the crutches. And he sprayed just the top of her cast, so it would feel lighter without floating away.

Asha sighed with relief and began walking with ease. Oscar put the bottle of repellent in his pocket to make sure he could help her walk home again later.

They made it to the path to the caboose in record time. Thanks to the gravity repellent, Asha was moving almost as quickly as she had before she broke her leg. And Oscar didn't trip once, even though he hadn't used any repellent on himself.

Getting into the clearing was trickier. Oscar sprayed more repellent on Asha's cast and held her crutches as she made her way down the hill. She walked like a crab on her hands and one good leg, letting her cast float out in front of her. When the cast got caught in vines, Oscar untangled it. Eventually they pushed through the shrubs and into the clearing.

Suddenly, they heard laughter and shouting coming from near the big tree. Oscar and Asha peeked around the corner and saw Zach and his friends crouched on the ground, drinking soda and throwing sticks at each other. The caboose was only about twenty feet behind them, but they didn't seem to have noticed it hidden under the vines.

Still, Oscar couldn't stand the fact that the boys had found their way into the clearing and were right next to their precious treasure. He looked at Asha and knew she felt the same way. Their hearts were in their throats as they watched the older boys shout and laugh and toss empty soda cans on the ground.

A bird sang in the branches above the boys' heads, and Zach threw a can at it. "Shut up, I'm trying to think!" he yelled at the bird, making his friends laugh.

"Doubtful," Asha whispered, rolling her eyes.

Another bird sang out, this time from the direction of the caboose. Zach threw another can of soda — a full one this time. The can struck the train car, and soda exploded in a burst of brownish foam against its side. Oscar and Asha both held their breath as they watched from around the tree trunk.

"What was that?" Zach said, standing up.

"They're going to find it!" Asha whispered frantically.

Oscar's chest grew tight as he watched Zach amble toward the caboose. A sick feeling grew in the pit of his stomach.

Zach grabbed one of the vines that Oscar had carefully pushed over the train car. He pulled, harder and harder, until the vine came loose. The bully fell over backwards, laughing. His friends stood up and started pulling on the vines too. Soon the side of the caboose was fully exposed, and Dr. Oopsie's mustached face stared out at the boys.

"Look!"

"Whoa!"

"Dude!"

The bully and his friends threw their half-finished soda cans into the weeds and started running around the caboose, trying to find a way into it.

Oscar and Asha stayed crouched behind the tree trunk. They didn't want to see what the boys would do, but they were afraid to look away and leave their treasure unguarded.

Zach climbed up the steps at the far end of the caboose.

"I hope the big spider bites him!" Oscar whispered a little too loudly.

"Shhhh!" Asha whispered. "Maybe he'll get frustrated with the latch, and they'll all give up and go home."

Zach pushed and pulled at the latch but couldn't get it to budge. He stood on his tiptoes and peered into the high window. The other boys gathered along the side of the caboose and watched their leader at the other end. Finally Zach hopped down to the ground. For a moment, he didn't say anything.

"What's he doing?" Oscar whispered.

"I don't know," Asha replied.

"Dude, this thing is lame," Zach said at last. "There's nothing in there; it's totally empty."

The other boys looked disappointed, but they all seemed to believe him. Not one of them tried to get past Zach to look in the window.

"Hey, Taylor," Zach said to one of the other boys, "didn't you get a new game for your XBox? Let's go to your house and play it."

The other boys shrugged, mumbling to each other that it sounded like a good idea. As Zach walked away, he picked up a rock and threw it at the picture of Dr. Oopsie, hitting him in the mustache. The others followed him out of the clearing. No one even glanced back at the caboose.

Asha sighed with relief. She struggled a bit with her crutches as she stood up. "Spray me with some more repellent," she said. "I'll need it to get this dumb cast up the steps."

Oscar didn't answer. He was too busy watching the gap in the shrubs where Zach and the others had disappeared.

"What are you waiting for?" Asha asked. "They're gone."

Oscar shook his head. "Something isn't right. Zach looked in that window for too long," he said, his eyes narrowing.

"What are you talking about?" Asha asked, sounding bewildered.

"Shh," Oscar whispered. "Just wait. Wait and watch."

Oscar remained perfectly still for several minutes, watching the shrubs. Asha fidgeted next to him and tried to make her leg more comfortable. Finally, they both heard a rustling in the shrubs, and Zach's head reappeared.

"I knew it!" Oscar gasped.

He and Asha watched, wide-eyed, as Zach walked back into the clearing and circled the caboose. He climbed up the stairs in the back again and pushed and pulled at the latch. He shoved and kicked at the door. Oscar jumped at the noise. Zach kicked harder, and Oscar heard the wood begin to splinter.

Oscar felt sick as he watched Zach pound at the door again and again with his feet and fists. After several shoves, Zach stopped and rubbed his hands, wincing. He jumped down off the end of the caboose and began looking around on the ground. Eventually he picked up a few potato-sized rocks, pulled his arm back, and took aim at the high window in the door. The first rock bounced off, but the second hit the glass, creating a big crack in it. Zach tossed the biggest rock from hand to hand a few times, as if deciding how to aim it.

"Oh no, you don't!" Oscar whispered. He decided to take action using the only thing he knew would work — the repellent. His heart was pounding in his ears as he took the bottle out of his pocket.

Asha looked at Oscar and then down at the bottle. She shot him a concerned look. "What are you going to do?" she whispered.

"I'm going to stop him!" he whispered back. "I can't sit here and do nothing!"

Oscar slowly crept over to a bush a few feet away from where Zach stood and crouched down behind it. He felt a flame of anger licking up the back of his neck. He grasped the spray bottle's nozzle in his right hand, readying himself for the attack.

Zach took half a step backward, aimed the rock carefully at the high window, and threw it. The rock went straight through the glass with a loud *SMASH!* and Zach whooped with satisfaction.

Oscar and Asha heard glass shatter inside the caboose as well and exchanged a horrified glance. The rock must have hit the display case.

Zach picked up another rock, walked around to the side, and took aim at the high window above Dr. Oopsie's face.

The flame up the back of Oscar's neck turned white-hot. Enough was enough. He unscrewed the nozzle cap from the bottle as he stood up.

"Oscar, *don't*!" Asha screamed. But it was too late.

Oscar pounced on Zach from behind and emptied the entire bottle over him, wetting his hair, T-shirt, shorts, and shoes. Some of the repellent splashed on Oscar's pants, and he grabbed a nearby bush and held on tight as his legs flew up in the air. Zach grabbed one of Oscar's legs and held on as he too floated up into the air.

Oscar turned his head over his shoulder and looked the bully straight in the eye. There was panic and fear on Zach's face as the repellent dripped down into his eyes. He seemed too startled and terrified to say anything.

Oscar kicked and thrashed his legs until Zach let go. The force of Oscar's kicks sent the bully flying upward *fast*. Zach panicked and moved his arms and legs at once, just like the spider had.

But unlike the spider, Zach had nothing to grab onto. He floated up past the caboose and then past the branches of the big tree. Finally he began to scream as a gust of wind carried him over the top of the tree and out of sight.

~Chapter 17~

Oscar couldn't look at Asha. He felt her eyes on him from across the clearing and knew he'd done a terrible thing. And yet, there was a part of him that was glad he'd done it. Zach had needed to be stopped.

Oscar floated upside down, legs up in the air, one hand clutching the bush that kept him from flying up after Zach. He stared at the empty bottle in his hand. The creak of Asha's crutches made him look up.

Asha stood in front of him with tears in her eyes. "Why did you do that?" she whispered.

Oscar looked past her, unable to meet her eyes. He shrugged and looked back down at the bottle, and they were both quiet. "I had to," he said finally. "You saw him. He was going to break into the caboose and ruin everything in it. Or steal stuff. And we haven't even seen it all yet." Tears filled Oscar's eyes, and he blinked fast to keep them from spilling out.

"But what will happen to him now?" Asha wondered out loud. She looked very worried.

Oscar's shoulders moved in a tiny, helpless shrug. "He'll float and . . . and fly until . . . until he . . ."

Neither of them wanted to finish the sentence. They knew what could happen when all the repellent finally evaporated, and they didn't want to imagine where Zach might be when it did.

"What should we do?" Asha asked.

"I don't know," Oscar muttered miserably.

"Well, we have to do something," Asha insisted. "We can't just pretend it didn't happen. We could tell the police. Or maybe the fire department. They have big ladders, and maybe they could help . . . um . . ."

"But then we'd have to tell them about the repellent," Oscar said quietly.

Asha was quiet for a moment, but then she nodded in agreement. "If we don't want anyone to find out about it, *we* have to rescue him," she said finally.

"But we don't know where he is," Oscar said. His legs drifted down to the ground, and he stood up.

"We know how the stuff works," Asha said, "so we know better than anyone else where he might end up."

Oscar looked at his feet and didn't say anything for a moment. Then he nodded. "We'll need flashlights," he said, looking up at the sky. "It might be dark before we find him."

Asha nodded and took a deep breath. Oscar brushed himself off, and together they headed out of the clearing.

On the way home, Asha struggled a bit with her crutches and walked very slowly. Oscar felt terrible — he had no more repellent with him to help her.

* * *

When they got back to Oscar's house, he and Asha each grabbed a flashlight. Oscar refilled the spray bottle using the second bottle of gravity repellent. As he poured the liquid from one container to the other, he thought, *I can't believe I wasted a whole bottle on that kid. Stupid me.*

Asha brought up a local news website on the computer and scanned the headlines. "Nothing about Zach," she said. "I guess no one has seen him."

"Maybe they did see him, but they don't care because they know he's a jerk," Oscar said.

"That's not funny, Oscar!" Asha cried. "You can make jokes once we know he's safe but not before then."

Oscar stared at the computer screen and said nothing.

Asha found a map of their town in an old phone book. They ripped it from the book, found a pen, and went outside.

Oscar drew a star near where Zach had left the ground. Asha licked her finger and held it up in the air to test which side the wind made coldest. Then she drew arrows on the map in the direction the wind seemed to be blowing. They circled the area the arrows pointed to, southeast of the clearing.

The sun was beginning to set, and the clouds were turning pink near the horizon. They would be out of daylight soon. Oscar sprayed gravity repellent lightly under Asha's arms and over the top of her cast to help her walk. Then he stuffed the flashlights and the spray bottle in his backpack, and they started off in the direction they hoped would lead them to Zach.

* * *

As Oscar and Asha walked through an unfamiliar neighborhood on the other side of the clearing, different thoughts bounced around in Oscar's head. *I know I have to help him*, he thought, *but I don't actually want to. If someone is always mean, why can't other people be mean back to him? Why should I have to be nice?*

Just then, Oscar remembered something his grandmother had said once about giving someone a taste of their own medicine. The expression hadn't made sense to him until now.

Zach wouldn't try to rescue someone he hurt, Oscar thought. *He'd probably just leave them there.*

Oscar walked more slowly as he thought about this.

Asha noticed him falling behind her on the sidewalk. "What's wrong?" she asked.

"What would Zach do?" Oscar said.

Asha looked confused. "What do you mean?"

"If Zach did this to me, he wouldn't try to rescue me," Oscar said. "He would probably just laugh and run away with his friends and let me float away . . ." he trailed off.

Asha walked back to where he was, and looked him straight in the eye. "But Zach is a bully," she said.

"Exactly," Oscar said. He crossed his arms in front of his chest. "So why should we bother helping him?"

Asha leaned on her crutches and looked right at him. "Because *we're* not mean," she said. "We won't do what Zach would do, because we're nicer than he is."

Oscar thought about this for a moment and kicked at the curb with his foot. He still wasn't convinced. "But does he *deserve* our help?" he asked.

Asha looked at him with concern. "Oscar, you dumped *all* that repellent on him, knowing what might happen." She searched his face for a reaction. "That was a mean thing to do, and I know you felt bad as soon as you did it!"

"But he was about to break into our caboose!" Oscar cried. "He'd already broken the window and . . . he was . . . "

"I know," Asha said quietly. "But you didn't have to use the whole bottle."

Oscar kicked the curb harder, then crouched down and hung his head. *It would be so easy to go home, eat dinner, play with the repellent and my* Star Wars *figures, and go to bed*, he thought. But he felt Asha's eyes on the top of his head.

"He could be really hurt, you know," Asha said. "And we might be the only ones who can help him."

Oscar raised his head. He pictured Zach lying under a tree with a broken leg, looking as helpless as Asha had a week before. He imagined himself walking away from Zach and laughing, and he thought it would make him feel good. But instead he felt a little sick to his stomach.

If I don't help Zach, Oscar realized, *then I'm no better than he is*. He'd done something wrong, and he had to try to fix it. As he sprayed more repellent on Asha to help her cope with her cast and crutches, Oscar realized he hadn't used any on himself all day — and he hadn't tripped once.

～Chapter 18～

"Zach!" Oscar shouted as he and Asha walked purposefully down the street. The name felt strange and unwelcome in his mouth, like a bad-tasting vegetable he knew he had to eat. But he and Asha had been calling it for more than an hour as they shone the flashlights up into trees and over the roofs of houses.

A man standing outside watering his lawn heard them shouting. "Who are you kids looking for?" he called out.

Oscar and Asha glanced at each other quickly as they walked over to the man.

"It's my cat," Asha said. "He loves to climb trees, and sometimes he gets stuck in them."

"Well, good luck. I hope you find him," the man said. "If I find a cat in a tree, I'll see if it answers to 'Zach.'"

Oscar giggled as the man walked away, and Asha poked him with her crutch.

As they walked to the outer edges of the neighborhood, the houses became farther apart, and the sidewalk eventually disappeared. They stopped when the paved street underfoot became a dirt road. Up ahead, Oscar could see a handful of houses and trees, but only one or two dim lights on front porches broke up the darkness.

"Oscar, I have to go back," Asha said. She balanced on one foot and rubbed under her arms, which were sore from her crutches, despite the gravity repellent. "The library will close soon, and I have to go there before I go home. I can't lie to my mom."

Oscar nodded. "It wasn't your fault, anyway," he said. "You shouldn't have to rescue him." He took the repellent out of his backpack and sprayed some more on Asha to make her walk home easier.

"Will you be okay by yourself?" Asha asked.

"Yeah, I'll be fine," Oscar replied. "I'll tap on your window when I get back."

Asha pointed her flashlight straight at him, and he squinted and tried to shield his eyes. "Don't stop until you find him," she said.

He sighed and nodded. Then Asha started back up the street, and Oscar and his flashlight beam disappeared down the dirt road.

Oscar had never really been afraid of the dark before, but he had also never been surrounded by this much darkness — especially not by himself. The sun had set, and the tiny sliver of moon didn't provide much light. The trees and unlit houses on the road were the same color as the black sky, so he couldn't see them until he swept over them with his flashlight.

Oscar could hear his heart beating in his ears. He decided then and there that quiet darkness was much scarier than loud darkness. When it was this quiet, little noises became much, much bigger. A twig snapped under his foot, and it sounded like a monster chomping on a bone. Oscar accidentally kicked a pebble along the road, and the *POCK-PUH-POCK* sound it made as it bounced made him jump.

But then another noise sounded in the dark — a whimper. Oscar was embarrassed to think that he'd made the noise. He looked around to make sure no one had heard him, and realized how silly it was to be self-conscious when he was clearly alone.

Then he heard the whimper again. It wasn't him! Oscar shined his flashlight around him but saw nothing.

The next whimper came from somewhere overhead. Oscar shined the flashlight upward and saw the branches of a big tree on his left. It was spindly and sharp looking and didn't have the thick leaf cover of the tree in his backyard.

"Here!" the whimper said.

Oscar's flashlight beam found a foot high up in the tree. The foot connected to a leg, which connected to a torso, which connected to a boy's face — Zach! Oscar barely recognized him. The bully's face was red and puffy, like he had been crying for hours.

"Who is that?" Zach called out in a shaky voice. "Can you help me?"

Oscar hesitated. Zach couldn't see him unless he shined the light on himself. He switched the flashlight off and thought for a moment. *What if I help Zach get out of the tree, but then he beats me up? Or steals my flashlight and leaves me here in the dark? Or what if he wants revenge for what I did to him, and he gets his friends together and they gang up on me?*

But the puffy eyes and red, tear-streaked cheeks didn't seem to want revenge. It wasn't a bully Oscar saw in the tree — it was a scared kid who had no idea what had happened to him.

"Hello?" Zach called out, sniffling and hiccuping. "Are you still there?"

Zach sounded so frightened, Oscar decided he should reassure him a bit.

"I'm here," Oscar said. He made his voice sound as deep as possible, so Zach wouldn't guess it was him right away. "Hold on a second."

Oscar knew he had to use the gravity repellent to help Zach get out of the tree, and Zach would want an explanation of what it was and where it had come from. If Oscar didn't help him, Zach might tell the police what had happened, and they would *definitely* demand an explanation.

Oscar thought he now understood another of his grandmother's sayings — he was stuck between a rock and a hard place.

As Oscar weighed his options, Zach continued to whimper in the branches overhead. Oscar decided to do something that was either very brave or very stupid. He wouldn't know which until the next day.

Oscar sprayed his shoulders, stomach, and back with a light mist of repellent, then put the bottle in his backpack. He tucked the flashlight into his belt so the light would shine on what was above him. Feeling lighter with the repellent's help, Oscar climbed the tree easily and made his way up to the high branch where Zach was stuck.

When Zach saw Oscar's face, he turned even redder, but not from crying. His face became familiar and mean again. "You!" he cried. "What are you doing here?" He angrily rubbed his eyes and runny nose with the sleeve of his shirt.

Oscar took a deep breath. He decided to act tough, like he was in control, even though he was terrified. "Look, Zach," Oscar heard himself say, "you're stuck up here, and I can get you down. Do you want my help or not?" He was surprised at how strong he sounded.

"You're the stupid jerk who did this to me!" Zach cried. "Why should I trust you?"

He has a point, Oscar thought. Maybe he had to apologize in order to get Zach to trust him. The idea of apologizing to a bully made him angry. *Zach wouldn't apologize to me*, he thought.

But Oscar reminded himself that *he* was not a bully.

Taking a deep breath, Oscar said, "I'm sorry. I'm sorry I scared you."

When Zach heard this, his face did something interesting. His eyes continued to glare, and his mouth sneered. But his eyebrows lifted in surprise. His nose must have been confused, stuck in the middle, so it continued to run.

Oscar almost laughed at how funny Zach looked, but he decided that would be unwise. "I can help you down, Zach," he said, "but first you have to trust me."

Zach looked at Oscar and then at his own leg. He shifted it an inch and winced. It occurred to Oscar that he might be injured.

"Are you okay?" Oscar asked.

"I'm fine," Zach snapped. "It's just a sprained ankle."

Oscar took another deep breath and reminded himself to act like he was in control. "Let's get you out of this tree," he said firmly.

"How are you going to do that, loser?" Zach scoffed. "I'm bigger than you."

Oscar winced at being called both a jerk and a loser in the span of a few minutes, but he forced himself to look Zach straight in the eye. "Do you trust me?" he asked.

Zach glared at him. He sneered, then smirked, and then seemed to run out of mean faces to make. "I guess I don't have a choice, do I?" he said finally.

Oscar took a deep breath, unzipped his backpack, and took out the bottle of gravity repellent.

"AUUGH!" Zach cried, panicked. "Get that stuff away from me!" He tried to move away but shrieked in pain as his foot twisted.

Oscar waited for Zach to calm down and stop shouting. "It's okay," he said. "This stuff is only dangerous if you use too much. I put wayyy too much on you today."

Zach stared at the bottle. "What is it?"

Oscar still wasn't sure he could trust Zach with the repellent, so he decided to give him only as much information as he needed. "Watch," he instructed. He took off his backpack, sprayed it lightly with repellent, and let it float upward a few inches.

As Zach watched, his eyes widened and his jaw dropped. The corners of his mouth lifted into a tiny smile.

"See, it's safe if you only use a little," Oscar said. "If I spray it on you, gravity won't pull you down as much, and then you'll be able to get out of the tree without falling. When it dries, you'll float down to the ground."

"Where'd you get that stuff?" Zach asked, his eyes narrowing.

Oscar panicked. He couldn't risk telling Zach the truth. He decided that telling a big lie was okay in a situation like this one.

"My uncle invented it, and it's top-secret," Oscar said. He thought for another moment, pondering whether Zach would try to take the repellent away from him. Oscar decided to take a big risk in order to protect the caboose. "I'll give you this bottle to keep," he continued, "but you can't tell *anyone* about it." He didn't know if a bribe would work, but he couldn't think of what else to do.

Zach's eyes narrowed, and Oscar could tell the other boy was thinking about how much fun it would be to have a bottle of the repellent all to himself.

Finally, the bully shrugged. "Okay," he said.

Oscar hoped Zach believed the story about his uncle and that he wouldn't see the connection between the repellent and what Oscar was about to say next. He took a deep breath.

"If I'm going to help you and give you this bottle, I need you to promise me something else," Oscar said. He tried to sound stronger than he ever had in his life. "Leave that caboose alone. I found it, and it's *mine*."

Zach sneered. "Whatever. Just 'cause you saw it first doesn't mean it's *yours*. It's a free country."

Oscar's eyes narrowed as he thought fast about how to make Zach take him seriously. "If you go near it again," he said, "I'll tell my sister that I rescued you tonight and that you were *crying* when I found you. She goes to your school, and she'll tell everyone."

The sneer finally left Zach's face. His eyes moved back and forth, and he seemed to struggle to turn his face from scared to mean again. "Fine, loser," he muttered. "Just get me out of here."

Oscar's heart beat faster when Zach called him that word. The heat that had crawled up the back of his neck earlier that day returned. But this time he felt stronger — braver. He sat up tall and looked Zach straight in the eyes.

"STOP CALLING ME A LOSER!" Oscar shouted.

Zach leaned back and held up his hands in front of him. "Okay, okay! Chill."

Oscar took a deep breath. Zach hadn't exactly promised him anything, but he felt like he was in control, at least for the moment. "Ready?" he asked Zach.

The bully looked nervous, but he nodded. He winced as the first mist of gravity repellent hit his stomach, then relaxed as Oscar sprayed it lightly over his shoulders and back.

"Let go," Oscar encouraged. "I'll shine the light on you so you can see where you're going."

Zach let go of the branch. "Whoa!" he exclaimed as he floated away from the tree. He untangled his foot and grabbed it midair, screwing up his face in pain. "Now what?" he called out to Oscar.

"Don't move around too much," Oscar called back. "Wait for it to dry, and you'll land."

Oscar pointed the flashlight at Zach until he was sure he would land safely and then sprayed a small amount of repellent on himself. As Oscar pushed himself down out of the spindly tree, he realized he didn't hear Zach below him. That made him nervous.

Oscar landed gently and shone the flashlight around him. Zach was still there, leaning against the trunk of the tree. He held his left foot off the ground and made a face.

"I think I broke something," Zach said quietly. "It really hurts."

"Here," Oscar said. He sprayed some gravity repellent on the injured foot, and Zach's face immediately relaxed as the foot floated effortlessly several inches above the ground. Then he sprayed Zach's chest and back very lightly, so he would be lighter and could hop on his right foot more easily. When he was finished, Oscar put the repellent in his backpack, went to Zach's left side, and stood close to him. "I'll be a crutch."

Zach hesitated, then put his arm around Oscar's shoulder and leaned on him. Oscar was surprised to realize that Zach was only a few inches taller than he was. The bully had always seemed so much bigger.

The boys started up the dirt road, hobbling along in silence for a while. Finally Oscar said,

"Hey, Zach?" The name felt different coming out of his mouth now.

"Yeah?" Zach said.

"What was it like to fly?" Oscar asked. "I mean, before the stuff wore off?"

"It was all right," Zach said. "I saw some cool stuff up there. The thing is, though . . ." he trailed off and glanced at Oscar sideways.

"What?" Oscar asked.

"Well . . . I'm sort of afraid of heights," Zach admitted.

Oscar tried very hard not to laugh, but a giggle escaped as he tried to imagine a bully being afraid of anything.

"Shut up!" Zach cried.

Oscar cleared his throat to hide the last giggle. "I'm afraid of spiders," he admitted. He wasn't certain, but out of the corner of his eye, he thought he saw Zach nod.

The two boys continued to walk and hop in silence. After ten minutes, they reached a corner, and Zach pointed down the street to the right. "The hospital's that way," he said.

"How do you know?" Oscar asked. Thanks to all his broken bones, he'd been to the hospital many times himself. But he didn't know quite where it was.

"My mom works there as a nurse," Zach said.

Oscar raised his eyebrows. He couldn't imagine a bully having a mom, but the more he thought about it, the more obvious it seemed.

The two boys headed down the street toward the hospital. Zach didn't call Oscar a loser once during the entire walk there. But Oscar wasn't sure he actually knew his name. When they reached the hospital, Oscar left Zach standing at the door. "I hope your foot is okay," he said. He paused for a moment. "And . . . I'm sorry."

Zach nodded and lightly punched Oscar in the shoulder. Oscar decided that might be the closest a bully could get to actually apologizing.

Oscar reached into his pocket and pulled out the spray bottle of gravity repellent. He handed it to Zach and looked him in the eye. "You'll leave the caboose alone. Right?"

Zach nodded and put the bottle in the pocket of his jeans.

It was impossible for Oscar to know whether Zach was telling the truth, but he figured he had no choice but to hold up his part of the agreement. "Be careful with it," Oscar added. "You only need a tiny bit."

"Duh," Zach said. Oscar thought he saw him smile a tiny bit.

Suddenly Oscar realized he had a problem: What was Zach going to tell people about his foot? How would he say he'd injured himself?

"What are you going to tell people about this?" Oscar asked, pointing at Zach's left foot.

Zach shrugged. "Don't worry about it, dude," he said, as he hopped through the sliding doors into the emergency room.

~Chapter 19~

Oscar walked back to his house, but before he went inside, he went next door and knocked softly on Asha's bedroom window. She was inside sitting on her bed, and she reached over to open the window as soon as she heard him.

"So?" she whispered through the screen.

"I found him! He was stuck in a tree," Oscar whispered.

"And?"

"And he's okay, I think. He hurt his foot, but I walked him to the hospital."

Asha's eyes widened.

"No, it was actually fine," Oscar said. "Well, not fine. He yelled a lot, but then I helped him get down. It's hard to explain, but by the end he didn't seem to be that mad at me."

"But is he going to tell on you?" Asha asked.

"I don't think so," Oscar replied. He thought for a moment, then shook his head. "But I don't know for sure. I think I did everything I could do, and now I just have to wait and see what happens."

Asha looked concerned. "I hope he doesn't want revenge," she said.

Oscar shivered at the thought, but he decided to try not to think about it too much. He changed the subject. "Did you get in trouble for being gone so long?" he asked.

"No," said Asha. "I came home with a couple of books. Will you be in trouble for being late?"

Oscar shook his head. "I don't think so. I'll just tell them I hurt myself, and I had to walk home really slowly."

Asha looked him up and down. "But you don't look like you hurt yourself," she said. "You're not a mess like usual."

Oscar smiled. "I didn't trip once today," he said proudly.

"Yeah, but you need to *look* like a mess so they'll believe you," Asha pointed out.

Oscar took a few steps away from the window and threw himself down on the ground. He rubbed one knee in the dirt and piled dry leaves on top of his head. He hooked his sleeve around a thorn on the bush next to him and pulled until the sleeve gave way with a loud *RRRRIP!* As the sleeve tore, Oscar really did fall backward, right into the same dirt he'd just smeared on his knee.

Asha watched him toss himself around and laughed. She heard her father calling her and stood up to close the window. "Sleep well, Oscar!"

"I doubt I will, but I'll try," he replied as he headed back to his own house.

As he walked through the front door, he remembered to limp. His story about injuring himself, combined with the dirt on his pants and his torn sleeve, convinced his parents. He felt bad for not telling the whole truth so soon after Asha's accident, but he figured rescuing a bully from a tree probably made up for it.

Later, as he pulled the leaves out of his hair and brushed his teeth, Oscar realized he hadn't told Asha that he'd given Zach the repellent. *What was I thinking*, he wondered, *bribing a bully like that? And how do I know that threatening to tell Gretchen that he cried will actually work?*

Oscar was terrified that by giving Zach the repellent, he had unleashed something awful on the other kids the bully liked to pick on. After several hours of tossing and turning, he finally fell asleep. But even then, he was haunted by images of kids flying off the playground monkey bars into space, and Zach shouting, "See ya, snotbrain!" as he pushed them.

* * *

Asha looked as tired as Oscar felt when they met on the front sidewalk the next morning.

"Did you sleep?" she asked.

"Not really."

"I didn't either," Asha replied.

"I kind of don't want to go to school today," Oscar said.

"Yeah, me neither," Asha said. Oscar raised his eyebrows. Asha normally loved school, so she must have been as worried as he was if she didn't want to go.

Oscar sighed heavily. "I guess we might as well get it over with," he said. He looked at her crutches. "Hey, isn't your dad driving you?"

Asha shook her head. "I feel like walking," she said. "After last night, I'm getting pretty fast."

Oscar had taken out the last bottle of gravity repellent and emptied it into another spray bottle. He put some on Asha to help her walk with the crutches, then took the bottle back inside and stashed it in his room. He decided to try his luck going without it.

Besides, Oscar thought, *if Zach and all his friends want to gang up on me, no amount of gravity repellent will help.*

Oscar and Asha started walking to school. He held his breath as they came around the corner where Zach and his friends normally hung out. The boys were all in their usual spots, shouting and hollering.

Oscar watched them closely as he approached to see if any of them were floating or moving in a strange way. Zach's left foot was in a big black boot-thing with straps across the top, but otherwise nothing looked out of the ordinary.

The other boys looked at Oscar as he approached, nudging each other and laughing. Zach looked up and saw them, and Oscar and Asha braced themselves.

"Hey, snotbrain!" said one of the boys. "Are you still a piggy bank? 'Cause I wanna go buy a soda, and I need some change."

Oscar rolled his eyes. Having confronted Zach last night, he'd realized these other boys weren't so scary anymore either. His heart beat a bit faster, but his throat didn't feel tight.

Oscar glanced at Zach to see if he was going to say anything, but Zach just looked off into the distance, ignoring what his friend had said.

Even though his hands were starting to shake, Oscar decided to be bold. He walked right up to the boy and stood as tall as he could. "Get your own stupid change, and *don't* call me snotbrain!" he said.

For a few moments that felt like an eternity, no one said anything. The boys stared at Oscar, and Oscar stared back. At last, Zach broke the silence.

"Yeah, man, why should this dude buy you a soda? He's not your *mom*," Zach said. The other boys laughed, and the one who had teased Oscar looked embarrassed.

Oscar didn't say anything else. He wanted to look at Zach to see if they had an understanding after the previous night, but he didn't know if that was a good idea in front of the other boys. Instead, Oscar turned away and continued on to school, gesturing for Asha to go in front of him.

As Oscar passed Zach on the sidewalk, he braced himself, just in case the bully said or did something to him. But Zach just nodded and said, "Later, dude."

Oscar looked straight ahead and said, as calmly as he could, "Later."

As Oscar and Asha walked away, they heard Zach's friends ask him how he hurt his foot. Zach started describing an epic stunt he did on his skateboard as his friends ooh-ed and aah-ed.

"That was weird," Asha said after a moment.

"Really weird," Oscar agreed. "But in a good way."

They walked the rest of the way to school in relieved silence. Oscar had a feeling that he'd been bullied by Zach for the last time, and that he'd never see him or the other boys in the clearing again.

* * *

That day in gym, Oscar and Asha's class played kickball. When it was Oscar's turn to kick, the ball flew straight out from his foot, and he made it to first base.

For most kids, this wouldn't have been an accomplishment. But Oscar did it without tripping and falling, which he had never managed to do before. He had daydreamed about this scene many times, and in his imagination, his classmates had cheered for him as he ran to the base in slow motion. What really happened wasn't nearly as exciting — no one seemed to notice at all.

But maybe that's a good thing, Oscar thought to himself.

As he stood on first base waiting for the next kid to kick, Oscar glanced up at the bleachers and saw Asha sitting there, her crutches beside her. She smiled at him, remembering, as he did, that he hadn't put on any gravity repellent that morning.

* * *

After lunch, Asha passed Oscar a note.

What else is in the caboose?

Oscar wrote back:

LET'S FIND OUT TODAY AFTER SCHOOL

They passed notes back and forth for the rest of the afternoon, mostly drawings of items they imagined were hidden in the old train car.

INSTANT MATH HOMEWORK (JUST ADD WATER!)

BULLY REPELLENT (new & improved sixth-grade formula!)

LEGO MULTIPLIER (MAKES AS MANY AS YOU WANT! AMAZE YOUR FRIENDS!)

EXTRA FINGER (when you need a spare!)

Oscar watched the second hand on the clock, which was moving painfully slowly as he waited for the school day to end. He and Asha couldn't wait to get back to Dr. Oopsie's weird and fascinating laboratory to see what other wonders awaited them.

About the Author

Tina L. Peterson has been fighting gravity her whole life. She was never any good at making balls go where she wanted them to on the playground, and she skinned her knees a lot. The idea for Oscar's tale first took root many years ago, when Tina saw a truck labeled "Gravity Services" parked in front of the house. She never did figure out what that truck was doing, but ever since that day, her imagination has played with the idea of turning gravity off, even if only for a little while. Tina has a PhD in mass media and communication from Temple University and is on the board of directors of the National Association for Media Literacy Education. Originally from Boulder, Colorado, she currently lives in Texas with her husband.

About the Illustrator

Xavier Bonet is an illustrator and comic-book artist based in Sant Boi de Llobregat, a town located near Barcelona, Spain. He began his career working with 2-D illustration and animation techniques and has worked as both an animator and background artist for various production companies. Now focused on the world of children's literature and comics, he creates works full of colors, textures, and sensations, blending both traditional and digital tools. Xavier creates his works with magic, fantasy, and above all else, passion, always putting his own stamp on his illustrations.